EMMA PAGE

Cold Light of Day

WALKER AND COMPANY · NEW YORK

First published in the United States of America in 1984 by the
Walker Publishing Company, Inc.

This paperback edition first published in 1986.

ISBN: 0-8027-3153-8

Library of Congress Catalog Card Number: 83-40435

Printed in the United States of America

10 9 8 7 6 5 4 3 2 1

CHAPTER 1

The wind had veered in the night and blew now soft and warm from the south. In the garden of Manor Cottage, three-quarters of a mile from the village of Littlebourne, the snowdrops were out; fat spears of daffodils were pushing up under the ancient apple trees.

The garden was large and rambling and had stood neglected for some years before the Pictons bought the property eighteen months ago. The garden was enclosed on three sides by an old wall of rose-red brick, mantled with ivy. Here and there a self-sown tree had sprung up in the shelter of the walls and stood now strong and established. The Pictons' daughter, Emily, their only child, climbed the trees summer and winter, made her dens among the branches, perched up there unseen, watching folk walk by along the road to Littlebourne, or a car going past in the other direction to Cannonbridge, five miles to the south-west.

In the cottage kitchen, cosy from the heat of the old solid-fuel stove, restored now and refurbished, the Pictons were finishing breakfast. All three of them wore Fair Isle jerseys painstakingly hand-knitted by Mrs Picton.

Emily sat opposite her father. She was nine years old, short and sturdily built, with a bright darting eye and a look of lively curiosity. She finished her porridge and began to fold her table napkin.

'Is that all you're going to eat?' Leonard Picton said with reproof.

'I have to be at school early.' She assumed an air of importance. 'I have to give out paper for the geography test.'

Leonard glanced at the clock. 'You've plenty of time. Finish your breakfast properly.' Emily unfolded her napkin again and cut herself a slice from a densely-textured wholemeal loaf; she spread it with butter and honey.

On a shelf of the dresser a radio recited its morning litany. Leonard gave it half an ear as he ate his coarse porridge of mixed whole grains, filling and sustaining, with an agreeable nutty taste. He was a spare, bony man in his middle forties with sharp features, thin fair hair receding at the temples, long, straggling side-whiskers. He taught history at the College of Further Education in Cannonbridge.

He glanced across at his wife who was standing by the stove, staring out through the window. 'Any more coffee?' he asked.

Olive came out of her thoughts. She picked up the jug that was keeping warm on the side of the stove and carried it to the table. She poured the coffee, fragrant and dark, made from a mixture of roasted barley and dandelion roots. Her hands were red and rough, marked and scarred from old scalds and burns, cuts and blisters.

She was a plain woman, a few years younger than her husband. Her figure was thin and angular. She wore no make-up and her hair, a nondescript brown already tinged with grey, was drawn severely back into a scanty bun.

She was just entering the streaming stage of a cold; her husband and daughter were more or less over theirs. Not that any of them referred to the ailment as a cold, the Pictons didn't believe in colds. They spoke of the body's attempt to throw off accumulated poisons, they dosed themselves with herbal concoctions and fruit juices. But however they referred to it and however they treated it, the malady seemed to affect them in very much the same way as less enlightened sections of the populace.

In the middle of the radio's calm recital of slow-downs and hold-ups, lay-offs and lock-outs, run-downs and snarl-ups, Leonard's ear caught the words Wall Street. He sat arrested in the act of lifting his cup to his lips and listened with fixed attention. He began to frown fiercely. An overnight fall in Wall Street, sudden and sharp, acute concern in Tokyo, fears in London of what the day might bring.

Olive slid a sidelong glance at her husband. He drained his cup and banged it down on its saucer. He began to chew the inside of his lips, to make a series of grimaces, staring down at the tablecloth with its bold pattern of blue and white checks.

'Is that bad?' Emily asked with sharp interest. 'When Wall Street falls?'

He jerked his head up. 'It's bad for me. But there are plenty of folk that'll make a fancy profit out of it.' He frowned even more fiercely. 'At my expense—and the expense of others like me.'

Olive gave a sudden violent succession of sneezes and dabbed at her nose. 'More coffee?' she asked but Leonard shook his head. He pushed back his chair. Time to be gathering up his books and papers, pumping up his tyres. All three of them rode bicycles; Leonard regarded the private motor-car as the invention of the devil.

Emily folded her napkin again and jumped up from the table. She ran out of the kitchen and up the stairs to her bedroom. She ran a comb through her long tawny hair, gleaming from regular washing in rainwater drawn from the butt outside the back door. She tied her hair back with a ribbon and tugged on a woollen cap. No need for a scarf on this fine morning, so mild for late February.

As she thrust an arm into the sleeve of her anorak her keen ears caught a sound, the gate of the adjacent property, Eastwood, singing under the touch of a hand. Mrs Cutler, most probably, the Eastwood daily woman, arriving for her morning stint. But it was just possible it might be someone else, some harbinger of novelty or excitement.

She darted across to the window overlooking the front garden and the road, and saw that it was indeed Mrs Cutler, plump and puffing after her ride from the village. She had dismounted from her ancient bicycle and was wheeling it up the Eastwood drive.

Emily picked up her satchel and ran downstairs. Her father had vanished about his own concerns but her mother came with her to the door and stood for a moment administering her usual hotchpotch of reminders and admonitions.

Emily nodded energetically to register hearing and heeding. She sprang on her bicycle and rode off down the garden path. She jumped off to open the gate and then with a last wave sprang on again and sped away up the road towards Littlebourne school.

In the garden next door Mrs Cutler didn't bother hoisting herself up again on to her bicycle in order to negotiate the drive. She had reached an age at which it was less trouble to push the bike up to the house than to jerk herself on to the saddle for the sake of a few minutes. There was no rush. Her employer, Mr Elliott, was an easy-going young man, a bachelor, thank goodness, far easier to work for than any married woman with a falcon eye for dust and smears of grease—and the married woman's habit of glancing at the clock when the door opened to admit her cleaning woman.

Take it all round, Mrs Cutler thought, by no means for the first time, Mr Elliott and I suit each other very well. The best part of a year now since she'd started working at Eastwood; he didn't bother her and she didn't bother him. She'd worked for enough finicky and whimsical employers in her time to be keenly appreciative of that, to know its rarity and value.

Fifteen years now since her husband had died, five years since the last of her children left home. She was as happy and contented as she had ever been, certainly as well-off. No tetchy husband to run round after, no sulky, uncooperative teenagers to argue with. She moved her head in satisfaction at the thought.

She reached the house, a handsome Edwardian dwelling, and wheeled her bicycle round to the rear; she propped it up inside a garden shed.

Gavin Elliott was upstairs in the bathroom when he heard Mrs Cutler let herself in at the back door. She didn't have a key; Gavin unlocked the door for her when he first went downstairs in the morning.

He peered at his face in the mirror above the wash-basin. His skin was always pale but this morning it looked even paler than usual, in marked contrast to the blue-black of his hair, thick glossy hair he had inherited from his mother. He had a slight headache but he scarcely registered that; he often woke in the mornings with a mild headache. He was in the habit of drinking a fair amount of wine with his dinner, followed by brandy, a glass or two of whisky later. He stuck out his tongue before the mirror, pulled a face and measured himself a dose of health salts which he drank at a single gulp.

Back in his bedroom he pulled on the jacket of his dark, conservatively cut suit. He was tall and slimly built, and looked even slimmer in his business clothes. He was thirty-one years old, head now of the family firm of Elliott Gilmore, investment brokers and financial consultants, which had its main office in Cannonbridge. He had inherited the business three years ago on the death of his father, Matthew Elliott.

He paused in front of the wardrobe mirror and adjusted the set of his jacket, picked up a clothes brush and passed it over the fine smooth cloth. His father had been a stickler for a smart businesslike appearance, in his own person as well as in the person of everyone he employed, and Gavin, who had loved and admired his father, adhered to the old tenets. He crossed to the dressing-table and took his wallet, his watch and keys from a small drawer.

His head was beginning to feel better. He went rapidly downstairs, calling out a cheerful greeting to Mrs Cutler, a ritual enquiry after her health, as he went into the kitchen to snatch a piece of crispbread and swallow a cup of coffee. Mrs Cutler was busy in the sitting-room but he didn't bother to stick his head round the door, nor did she bother to come to the sitting-room door to answer him.

'I'm all right,' she called back, 'but I don't know for how long. I reckon I'm starting one of these nasty colds that are going round, I've got a bit of a throat this morning.' She continued to work as she spoke. She removed a little porcelain group from the top of a Georgian bureau and set it carefully down, out of harm's way. She began rubbing vigorously at the mahogany surface with a chamois leather. There were a lot of nice things in the room and in the house generally; she liked that, she liked working among nice things, enjoyed keeping them looking their best.

She carefully dusted the group—a shepherd and shepherdess with a pair of lambs at their feet—and replaced it in its correct position. Mr Elliott had inherited a lovely lot of porcelain from his mother, she seemed to have made a hobby of collecting it, but unlike some folk Mrs Cutler had worked for, who kept everything valuable locked away in cabinets, young Mr Elliott kept his treasures openly on display, to be enjoyed every day by himself and others.

She stood back and looked critically at the bureau, gave a nod of satisfaction and turned her attention to a Regency card table. She rubbed assiduously at the beautiful dark-veined rosewood; she knelt to deal more effectively with the intricately carved base, every line of her short stubby figure expressing energetic dedication to the task of bringing up the soft mellow shine. Her cheeks took on a rosy glow, her iron-grey hair began to stick stiffly out in wisps.

She paused for an instant as the phone rang in the front hall, then she resumed her vigorous polishing; it wasn't her duty to answer the phone when Mr Elliott was in the house.

In the kitchen Gavin swiftly despatched the last fragments of his crispbread and drained his coffee before going at a rush into the hall to pick up the receiver. He smiled as he recognized the high girlish tones at the other end.

'Charlotte! Hello!' he said with pleasure. He had met Charlotte Neale at a charity ball in the late autumn. She seemed to like him and he was quite certain he liked her. This could be the one, he'd decided almost at once—but take it easy, my lad, he'd told himself, don't rush it, don't wreck your chances at the start.

'This is just to let you know I definitely am off to Switzerland next week,' Charlotte told him. She was eighteen years old, the daughter of an old county family. Her father owned racing stables; he was well known as a sound judge of horseflesh and the breeder of some notable bloodstock. 'I'm off on Wednesday,' she added. There had been some talk of Gavin taking her to a race meeting the weekend after next. 'Sorry I won't be here for it,' she said. She was spending a few weeks with an old school friend and her family near Arosa.

'We could have dinner one evening before you go,' Gavin suggested. 'Monday or Tuesday?' They settled on Tuesday. 'But I mustn't be late getting back,' she told him. 'I'll have to be up very early on Wednesday to catch the plane.' The Neales lived at Berrowhill Court, seven or eight miles from Littlebourne.

Gavin glanced at his watch as he replaced the receiver. Time he was making tracks, it wouldn't do to be late at the office. He scrupulously followed his father's habit of always setting a good example, being at his desk spruce and ready to deal with business at the beginning of the day.

He didn't give Mrs Cutler any directions about her work before he left the house. She had been with him long enough to know what was needed. He had bought Eastwood after his father died, moving in some two and a half years ago. In the first eighteen months he lived there, before Mrs Cutler came to work for him, he had endured a succession of unsatisfactory daily women. He knew his luck in finding Mrs Cutler and he intended to hang on to her.

She came out of the sitting-room as he opened the front door. 'Look after that throat,' he said. 'We don't want you falling ill.'

She followed him outside to shake her dusters. 'Oh, I'll be all right,' she said cheerfully. 'I've got some lozenges to suck.'

Gavin walked round the side of the house towards the garage and backed his car out. As he drove down to the front gate he saw with irritation that his neighbour, Leonard Picton, was standing outside the gate, stiff as a ramrod, clearly waiting to speak to him.

Gavin made a sound of exasperation. He was beginning to find Picton a damned nuisance. When Gavin bought Eastwood, Manor Cottage stood empty. A year later the Pictons bought the cottage and Gavin went out of his way to be helpful and friendly to them. Picton had bought the property at a bargain price and he had a good slice of capital left over from the sale of his previous house; for the first time in his life he had money to invest.

He learned in the course of a casual chat in the roadway that Gavin was the head of a firm of investment brokers and he asked Gavin's advice about the investment of his capital — on a purely friendly, neighbourly level. And Gavin, on a purely friendly, neighbourly level, advised him — without the scrupulous care he would have given the matter if Picton had presented himself in the ordinary way as a client at the Cannonbridge office of Elliott Gilmore.

Always a man with a keen nose for a bargain, Picton was delighted with this free picking of Gavin's brains. He instructed his bank without delay to buy the stocks Gavin had suggested.

At first he was delighted with his purchases. Whenever he looked at the financial pages he found his stocks were steady or rising. Until a few months ago. Then they began to fall. He couldn't understand it, he was horrified. He waylaid Gavin in the road.

'No need to worry,' Gavin told him cheerfully. 'Always a bit of a gamble, the market, full of whims and moods. Just hang on, you'll find your shares will recover.'

But they hadn't recovered, they had continued to slide. Picton waylaid Gavin again. 'It's only a hiccup in the market,' Gavin assured him. 'You didn't buy in order to make a quick profit, they're a long-term investment. Forget them for four or five years. You'll be pleasantly surprised when you look at them again then.'

But Picton couldn't or wouldn't forget them. He continued to study the financial pages and the market continued to hiccup; the hiccups grew more violent. Picton's anxious enquiries turned to frowns, reproaches, finally to outright accusations of professional negligence. Gavin heartily wished he had never opened his mouth in the matter. The man was an idiot, he should have put his money in a building society and slept at nights; he didn't have the temperament for anything more adventurous.

There's nothing more I can say to him, he thought now with weary resignation as he approached the gate with

Picton planted firmly at the other side. He halted the car and stepped out on to the gravel. He bade Picton a civil good-morning and made to open the gate. Picton clung resolutely to it with both hands.

'Oh no you don't,' he said. 'You're going to stand there and listen to what I've got to say.' Gavin made no reply. He stood in a posture of total neutrality, his face wiped clear of expression.

'You've heard the news this morning,' Picton said with fierce intensity. Gavin shook his head. He hadn't listened to the radio and the village shop no longer delivered newspapers. 'Wall Street,' Picton added, seeing Gavin's uncomprehending look. 'Another slide, even bigger.' He darted his head forward suddenly, still maintaining his hold on the gate. Gavin couldn't prevent himself from stepping back a pace. 'It's not good enough,' Picton said on a louder note. 'You'll have to recompense me. For every penny I've lost.'

Gavin expelled a long breath of exasperation. He had already explained to Picton that he—and certainly not the firm of Elliott Gilmore—was in no way legally responsible for the success or failure of Picton's investments. He had also tried to make him perceive that a loss is never a loss until the stocks are sold. He most assuredly didn't intend to waste more time and energy going over the same ground again. He made a sudden lunge at the gate and managed to snatch it from Picton's grasp; he swung it open. He got swiftly back into his car and set it in motion, half expecting Picton to rush over and slam the gate shut again. But Picton made no move, he stood his ground. Gavin had a horrid notion that he wasn't going to budge, that he would be compelled to get out of his car again and manhandle him out of the way. He continued to inch the car forward.

At the last moment Picton suddenly stepped aside and Gavin was out through the gate. He felt a strong inclination to keep going and let the gate stand open till Mrs Cutler left. But Picton would undoubtedly see that as some kind of victory, so he halted the car and walked briskly back.

'Don't kid yourself this is the last you'll hear of it,' Picton said as he came up. 'I'll see you pay for what I've lost. One way or another.'

CHAPTER 2

Gavin didn't answer, didn't look at Picton. He closed the gate, turned and went back to his car. As he moved off he glanced in the mirror and saw that Picton was still standing by the gate, shouting after him, but he couldn't make out the words.

He frowned as he drove up the road. Until now he had considered Picton no more than a nuisance, he had laughed as he retailed the story of his encounters with Picton in the office. Now it seemed a good deal more serious, very far from a joke. The man's not entirely rational, he thought with a faint edge of anxiety; he'll go over the edge one day.

He dismissed the notion from his mind with a shake of his head and cast a glance at the day ahead. Friday, February 26th; the usual weekly meeting in the afternoon of the heads of the three Elliott Gilmore branches. He was himself in charge of the Cannonbridge office and his half-brother Howard, twelve years older, was in charge of Wychford, a smaller town ten miles to the west. The newest branch at Martleigh, a town smaller still, twenty-two miles to the north-east, had been open less than a year and was doing well, more than justifying its existence. The manager, promoted after long service in the Wychford office, had suffered from recurrent bouts

of gastric trouble during the autumn and winter. He had
at last gone into hospital for an operation and was at
present in Majorca, convalescing. In his absence the
branch was being managed by his number two, Stephen
Roche, who had worked at the Cannonbridge office
before going to Martleigh.

Yes, things were going pretty well; his father would
surely have been pleased with the way he'd run things
since he'd inherited. His youthful follies were all behind
him now; time to think about settling down, raising a
family, rearing a son to take over one day in his turn. The
idea was deeply satisfying. Charlotte, he thought again,
he'd have to go a long way to find someone more suitable
than Charlotte. Just give it time, it would all come to
hand. He began to hum a tune as he reached the outskirts
of Cannonbridge.

In the breakfast-room at Claremont, a graceful Queen
Anne dwelling a few miles to the west of Cannonbridge,
Howard Elliott and his wife Judith were finishing breakfast. Judith was meticulously groomed and carefully
dressed; no unexpected caller would find her looking less
than her best. She wore a beautifully cut housecoat of
heavy French silk the colour of almond blossom; it gave
her a delusive air of fragility.

She ate a little fruit and crispbread while Howard
despatched porridge and cream, bacon and eggs, toast
and marmalade; the breakfast he had always eaten in his
mother's day, the breakfast he would have been
astounded not to find presented to him punctually every
morning. He read his newspaper as he ate, he kept his
eyes on the paper as he pushed his cup across to Judith for
more coffee. She refilled the cup and gave it back to him
without speaking. She had learned very soon after her
marriage that it was a waste of breath trying to talk to
Howard over the breakfast-table.

He picked up his cup and took a drink without raising his eyes from his newspaper. Judith gave him a long dispassionate look. He was forty-three years old, a tall, heavily-built man who looked his age and more. His youthful good looks had coarsened, his figure was slipping from control.

He was the only child of Matthew Elliott's first marriage which had ended twenty years ago in an acrimonious divorce. At the time Howard was working in the family firm; it had always been taken for granted that he would one day succeed his father. But Howard was deeply upset at what he saw as his father's betrayal of his mother. He took his mother's side over the divorce and quarrelled bitterly with his father. He left Elliott Gilmore and found a post with another firm of financial consultants in a neighbouring town. He never again exchanged so much as a word with his father.

Now he drank the last of his coffee and pushed back his chair. He folded his newspaper and tucked it under his arm. He had lived at Claremont all his life, with his parents until their divorce and afterwards with his mother, until her death some two years ago. He had inherited nothing under his father's will, but Claremont and its furnishings, its pictures and objets d'art, had all been left to him by his mother, together with the substantial investments on which she had lived; she had received a very generous settlement at the time of the divorce. Whatever reasons she had for feeling bitter towards her husband—and she had continued to feel bitter towards him until the end of her life—a niggardly settlement certainly wasn't one of them.

Matthew had been a good husband to her but she had believed him to be a blameless one, totally loyal; she had regarded this as no more than her due. She was a woman without warmth of nature, preferring the word duty to the word love. After a few years of marriage she had finally closed the door of her bedroom on Matthew, intimating that with the approach of middle age—rather a distant approach as she wasn't yet thirty-five at the time—they were now, as she put it, past all that sort of thing.

But Matthew, only a year or two over forty, was very far from past it, he was in fact all for it, and certainly didn't intend going without it. He took care to be discreet in his adventures and no doubt the calm surface of his family life would have continued unruffled but that one day a couple of years later he fell suddenly and violently in love—something he hadn't bargained for.

He set up his new lady, a dark-haired, ivory-skinned beauty, warm-hearted and loving, in a secluded, charming little house at a safe distance from Claremont. He spent as much time with her as he could contrive. After a year or two Gavin was born. They both loved the child but there was no question of marriage; Matthew had made that very clear at the beginning.

But one day chance took a hand and the liaison came to light. Matthew's respectable, conventional family life blew up in his face. His wife offered him the immediate option of divorce or severing all contact, except for any necessary financial arrangement, with the dark-haired beauty and Gavin, by now eleven years old; she had no doubt which course he would choose.

All his business life Matthew had been faced with the necessity for making swift choices. This one took him thirty seconds. He chose divorce, to the outraged and vociferous astonishment of his wife. Immediately after the divorce he married his love. He sold the secluded little house and bought a larger property to the south of Cannonbridge, out of his ex-wife's immediate sphere of social influence. There he lived happily with his new family until the death of the dark-haired beauty ten years later.

When Matthew followed her after another seven years, neither Howard nor his mother attended his funeral. Without Matthew's solid existence to sustain her bitterness his first wife lost her vitality, her sense of focus on life, and slid quietly out of it twelve months after Matthew's funeral.

As soon as was decently possible Howard cast about for a suitable bride, someone to step into his mother's shoes, look after his creature comforts, see that his well-ordered, agreeable existence was in no way altered. Within a short time he found Judith, ten years his junior; he proposed to her without delay.

Shortly after the wedding his half-brother Gavin, anxious to heal the family breach and feeling that now, with all the principal adversaries dead, might be a propitious moment, approached Howard and asked if he would consider returning to Elliott Gilmore to run the Wychford branch. This was long-established, on a very sound and stable footing. After a good deal of thought Howard agreed; he had now been running the Wychford branch for eighteen months.

Now Judith stood up from the breakfast-table and followed her husband into the hall. She was a little over average height, with a slim, well-formed figure. Her looks were very English; fair hair well cut and disciplined, gleaming from regular attention at the best local salon; a fine, smooth skin, regular features, clear, blue-grey eyes.

'Friday today,' Howard said, sufficiently fuelled by now to be able to greet the new day with speech. 'I'll be over at Cannonbridge this afternoon for the meeting.' His lips brushed her cheek. 'I should be home around six. Are you doing anything today?'

'I'm out to lunch.' She mentioned the name of a female cousin of hers, married with a family, living several miles away. 'I'll be back well before you.' Something else that Judith had learned very soon after her marriage was that

Howard detested coming home to an empty, silent house.

She opened the front door and stood watching as he went off to his car. He turned and raised his hand in a ritual wave. She gave him a wave in reply, closed the door and stood with her back against it, contemplating the day ahead.

The main offices of Elliott Gilmore occupied a central position in an elegant early-Victorian terrace of shops and offices in the principal business area of Cannonbridge. There was no Gilmore now in the firm; old Matthew had bought out his partner's widow many years ago.

Gavin walked round from the car park and stood surveying the frontage. For some time he had been contemplating alterations and improvements to the main office. He had no intention of losing any of the period charm but it could be made a good deal more convenient and efficient, more economical to run.

Apart from occasional primping and decorating, the building was very much as it had been when Gavin first walked up the steps. Before his parents married he had had no idea what his father did for a living, apart from the vague information that he was engaged in business which compelled him to be away from home a good deal of the time.

One day shortly after his second marriage, Matthew took Gavin into Cannonbridge and in through the front door of Elliott Gilmore. He introduced him to the staff simply as 'my son Gavin'. He was well aware that they had all read the newspapers, they'd heard all the gossip, all the echoes of that fierce uproar, but he was also well aware that they all depended on him for their living. There would be no sly looks, no amused nudges—or at least not inside the building.

Gavin had been profoundly impressed by the grand air of the establishment, the pillared entrance, the wide

stretches of gleaming parquet, the tall windows and orna-
mental ceilings. Today, twenty years later, he still felt
pleasure in all these features as he walked up the front
steps and into the reception hall.

The offices were on two floors, with a third floor given
over to stockrooms, and a basement that had once housed
a gigantic boiler but was now virtually unused. No reason
why the basement couldn't be transformed into a stock-
room and the third floor turned into an additional office,
together with a staff rest-room and extra toilet facilities.

He walked slowly along the corridor to his office,
pondering various possibilities. A few moments later there
was a tap at the door and his secretary, Miss Tapsell,
came in with the morning post. She was a short, stocky
woman in her forties, resolutely settled into spinsterhood.
She always looked neat and businesslike in a dark tailored
suit and white blouse; her greying brown hair was parted
in the centre and drawn smoothly back into a French
pleat.

She had worked at Elliott Gilmore since leaving school.
Gavin had first met her on the day his father brought him
into the office. He had never known her in any other garb
or with any other hairstyle, although the grey was a recent
feature. She had been his father's secretary and Gavin
had been delighted to inherit her; she was loyal, hardworking and conscientious.

She had already been in the building for half an hour
this morning, she always came in early. She was still
bristling slightly from one of her set-tos with the office
cleaner, a lady whom she suspected of skimping her work,
arriving late and leaving early.

But none of this appeared on Miss Tapsell's face now,
as she came into Gavin's office; her manner, as always,
was calm and precise. She wouldn't dream of troubling
Mr Gavin with such a trifling matter, she would get it
sorted out herself in good time.

When Gavin had dealt with the post he went through the agenda for the afternoon's meeting with Miss Tapsell. 'A couple of points I'd better mention to Roche first,' he said when they had finished. 'Give him time to mull them over before the meeting. Get him on the phone for me, will you?'

The town of Martleigh was a good deal smaller than Cannonbridge but prosperous enough, with more than one long-established and solidly-based local industry. The Martleigh branch of Elliott Gilmore occupied the ground floor of a newish office block near the town centre.

Stephen Roche sat at his desk, studying a file of papers. He was in his late thirties, no more than average height, with a strong, wiry build. He had a broad, unlined forehead, eyes of a clear pale amber, sharply intelligent.

He always got to his office early, was often the first to arrive. He stayed in lodgings in Martleigh during the week, returning at weekends to his house on the edge of Cannonbridge. When he had first been sent to Martleigh twelve months ago he had commuted daily from Cannonbridge; he found the journey, twenty-two miles each way, just about tolerable.

But within a couple of months extensive roadworks, long promised, often postponed, were finally begun along a sizable stretch of the carriageway, causing unpredictable and time-consuming delays morning and evening. After a few weeks of being late for appointments and tensing himself every afternoon for the drive home with its lengthy queues and maddening hold-ups, Roche decided to abandon the struggle and look for digs in Martleigh. 'It won't be for long,' he told his wife. The Ministry officials were confident the traffic would be flowing normally long before Christmas.

But there was industrial trouble in the late summer,

and then, when that had been at last resolved, a spell of
severe weather, early and prolonged, in the autumn, with
all the consequent delays and interruptions to schedules.
It would probably now be Easter or even later before the
giant machines clattered away for the last time.

Roche glanced up now from his papers and his gaze fell
on the plain silver frame that held a photograph of his
wife. It stood on his desk, a little to one side, next to the
potted plant that his secretary kept assiduously fed and
watered. The photograph showed the head and shoulders
of a young woman with an unsmiling look, large, well-set
eyes, hair simply cut, with a slight wave. Roche frowned.
His secretary must have moved the photograph when she
attended to the plant; it was a little out of its usual place.

The phone rang suddenly on his desk. He picked up the
receiver and heard Gavin Elliott's voice. As he listened to
the details of the afternoon's agenda he stretched out a
hand and replaced the photograph in its exact customary
spot, where Annette's eyes would meet his own whenever
he glanced up from his work.

The Friday afternoon meeting finished a little earlier
than usual. It was just after four when the three men in
their dark suits came out of Gavin's office, followed by
Miss Tapsell who had as usual been taking notes.

Gavin would stay on at his desk for another hour or two
but Howard was going straight home, and so was Stephen
Roche. Both men always cleared up in their own branches
on Friday morning; the traffic and the distances involved,
particularly in Roche's case, made it not worth returning
there after the meeting. Gavin stood for a few moments
chatting to the other two before turning back into his
office.

Miss Tapsell glanced at the three of them as she went
off along the corridor. Roche with his sharp eyes and long
foxy muzzle; the two half-brothers, alike only in their

height, inherited from their father. Howard had also inherited Matthew's solid build and heavy shoulders, but he had his mother's light brown hair, her blue eyes and regular features. Good-looking enough in his way, Miss Tapsell used to think years ago, though beginning now to let himself go.

Always the cautious one, Howard, always wanting everything in writing, everything hedged against, triply guaranteed. Beside him Gavin looked far more handsome, with his slim build, the striking colouring he had inherited from his mother. More adventurous than his half-brother, always prepared to take a reasonable risk, but still with sound business instincts.

The two men seemed to be getting on a good deal better than Miss Tapsell had dared hope when Howard first returned to the firm; there had been moments when she had feared it had been a bad mistake. She liked to think that Matthew would have been pleased to see them together in the firm at last, on such easy, friendly terms.

Gavin went back into his office and Howard and Roche went out through a rear door into the car park. Howard made some comment on the mild weather and then went off to his car, a sleek, expensive saloon. He raised a hand as he moved out, past Roche stepping into his own vehicle, small and neat, nippy in traffic.

Roche drove out into the side-street and headed for the eastern edge of town. His house, Greenlawn, was a detached Edwardian villa standing in a large secluded garden that gave the property an air of rural tranquillity.

The afternoon was still washed over with pale sunshine as Roche halted the car and got out to open the gate. He ran the car up the sloping drive and brought it to rest by the front door. He took a suitcase and hand-grip from the boot and let himself into the house. He stood in the hall for a moment, listening.

No sound inside the house, no stir of movement. Only

the echoes of this false spring, with its summer-seeming sounds, the far-off slam of a car door, voices calling, the cries and laughter of children in some distant park, the muted bark of a dog, the hum of traffic from a trunk road half a mile away.

He went up the stairs and paused by the landing window. He set down his cases and stood looking out at the rear garden. At the far end, on the edge of the shrubbery, he could see the tall slender figure of his mother-in-law, Mrs Sparrey. She held a wooden trug, she was looking down at Annette who was on her knees close by, digging up a clump of some early-flowering plant. Annette levered up the plant and reached up to put it in the trug, no doubt for her mother to carry back to her own garden ten miles away.

Annette began an attack on another plant. Her chestnut hair swung forward, gleaming in the sunlight. Mrs Sparrey turned her head and glanced back at the house. Roche could see the olive of her cheek, the carefully coiffured lines of her steel-grey hair, strikingly curled back from her face in an elaborate sweep that nothing, not even the most unruly wind, ever seemed able to disturb.

He picked up his cases and went along to the main bedroom. As he set the cases down he caught sight of himself in the dressing-table mirror. A head of thick straight hair, very fair in childhood but now a commonplace brown. His eyes looked back at him with a detached gaze. He turned from the mirror and began to unbutton the jacket of his suit.

CHAPTER 3

Sunday morning continued mild with a slight breeze. The air was very clear today with a brilliant, sparkling quality. In the garden at Claremont the birds darted about with manic frenzy, calling, challenging, swooping and dipping, snatching up broken twigs, old grass, downy feathers.

Inside the house activity was a good deal less frenetic. Howard and Judith were both up—it was almost eleven—and were making a languorous onslaught on the debris of last night's dinner-party; Judith had made a start on the washing-up.

Howard was in the drawing-room. He confined his assistance to emptying ashtrays, plumping up cushions, picking up scattered petals from flowers that had failed to survive the evening. He paused by a window to twitch the long brocade curtains into place. Sunlight illumined distant stretches of farmland, wooded tracts still winter-dark. But he scarcely glanced at the view he had seen all his life.

He went along to the kitchen, fragrant now with the smell of freshly-made coffee. Judith was at the sink, rinsing a stack of plates under the tap. Howard poured the coffee, strong and reviving. Judith pulled off her rubber gloves and took an invigorating mouthful.

On a shelf near the kitchen door the telephone rang suddenly. Howard crossed the room and lifted the receiver. 'Oh—hello,' he said after a moment. 'How are you now? Feeling better?' He put a hand over the mouthpiece. 'Aunt Harriet,' he said. Judith set down her cup. 'That's good,' Howard said into the phone. 'Yes, Judith's here, I'll hand you over.'

Aunt Harriet—Mrs Fiske—was Judith's godmother, aunt merely by courtesy title. She lived in a village some sixty miles to the north of Cannonbridge; she was the widow of a wine importer. In a few days she would be celebrating her seventieth birthday. She had intended to give a dinner-party in honour of the occasion but two or three weeks ago she had taken to her bed with 'flu, she had been very unwell. She had been forced to cancel the dinner-party, but now it seemed it was on again.

'Yes, of course we'll come,' Judith told her. 'We'll be delighted.' Howard pulled a face. 'I'll come over a day or two earlier,' Judith added. 'If that's all right with you. Thursday morning?' The dinner-party was on Saturday. 'Howard can drive over after work on Friday.' She glanced up at him and he moved his shoulders to signify grudging acquiescence.

By Tuesday evening it was beginning to turn cold again. The forecast was for overnight frost and an easterly wind in the morning. Gavin sat opposite Charlotte Neale in the well-appointed dining-room of the Caprice, a restaurant renowned for its cooking, situated half a mile out of Cannonbridge.

'Do have something else,' Gavin urged her when she had finished a rich creamy dessert. 'Some cheese? Fruit?'

She shook her head. 'No, thanks, just some coffee.' She glanced up at the clock. 'I don't want to be much later.'

As they drank their coffee she chatted about the friend she was going to stay with in Switzerland. She was looking forward to some skiing. 'There's still plenty of good snow,' she said, smiling with pleased anticipation. She showed not the slightest sign that she would miss him.

He stirred his coffee, feeling a little melancholy. Don't rush it, he warned himself again, don't spoil it before it starts. He looked at her across the table; the lovely heart-shaped face; thick flaxen hair, taken up this evening into a casual knot on top of her head; peach skin; eyes the soft deep blue of lobelias.

But it wasn't just her looks, it was her attitude, her whole approach to life. Open and direct, no come-ons or put-offs, no airs and graces, no coquettish nonsense. No past, no complications.

He raised his cup to his lips. At the back of his throat he could feel an unpleasant roughness. He knew the feeling of old. Oh hell, he thought, I believe I'm getting Mrs Cutler's cold. She had appeared at Eastwood as usual that morning but she had looked flushed and unwell. 'I do feel pretty rotten,' she said when he questioned her. 'If I don't come tomorrow it'll mean I've decided to have a day or two in bed. I'll be back as soon as I can.' As he'd left for work he'd heard her coughing and blowing her nose.

The air was sharp as he drove Charlotte back to Berrowhill. 'I won't ask you in,' she said as she got out of the car. 'They'll only start talking to you, and I want to get to bed.' The sky was thickly clustered with stars. From the stables came the stir of horses, the voice of a stable lad.

Gavin walked with her to the door. 'Write to me,' he said. 'Let me know how you get on.'

She made a little face. 'I hate writing letters.'

'You could phone.'

She moved her shoulders.

'Don't forget me,' he said. As he bent his head to give her a light kiss he gave a sudden violent sneeze. She jumped back.

'I'd rather you didn't kiss me,' she said with energy. 'I don't want to start my holiday with a streaming cold.'

By Friday morning Gavin's cold was turning feverish. Mrs Cutler hadn't shown her face at Eastwood since Tuesday, she was presumably nursing herself at home in her cottage.

It was a raw, chilly morning. Gavin shivered as he came out of the house and walked to the garage, although he had wrapped himself up with care. I'll be glad when today's over, he thought as he drove into Cannonbridge. Not only was there the usual list of appointments in the morning and the weekly meeting in the afternoon, but, worst of all, he had to attend a dinner in the evening over at the Northgrove Hotel. Northgrove was a small township which stood at the apex of a triangle with Cannonbridge and Martleigh at either end of the base line; it was roughly equidistant from both places.

The dinner was being given by the Northgrove Chamber of Commerce and was typical of many functions Gavin attended in the course of a year. In the ordinary way he didn't dislike these occasions; sometimes they were quite enjoyable. But to sit through one feeling as he did now — not a cheerful prospect.

He walked slowly up the front steps of Elliott Gilmore and into the building. His head felt woolly and his legs far from steady. It was beginning to seem a good deal more like 'flu than a cold. He had breakfasted on black coffee and aspirin and he intended to repeat the dose throughout the morning. The thing is to buckle down to work and forget about how you feel, he told himself bracingly as he went into his office. With luck the aspirins would have some effect and by evening he would be feeling less like death warmed up.

By midday, when he terminated his last appointment as speedily as he could without overt rudeness, he was feeling very poorly indeed. 'You don't look at all well,' Miss Tapsell said with concern as she removed yet another empty coffee cup from his desk. 'I really think you should give in and go home to bed.' He began to shake his head. 'I'll phone Mr Howard and Mr Roche,' she said with resolution. 'I'll explain that you're not well, you've had to go home, there won't be a meeting this afternoon. They won't mind. There's nothing urgent on the agenda, it can all stand over till next week.'

He looked up at her. 'It's this dinner at Northgrove. If I go to bed now I'll never be able to force myself to get up again this evening.' At the thought of having to struggle into a dinner-jacket and drive over to Northgrove, sit through an interminable meal and endless speeches, he could have dropped his head into his hands and groaned. 'I can't cry off at such short notice.'

'I shouldn't let that worry you,' Miss Tapsell said robustly. 'Either Mr Howard or Mr Roche will go in your place, I'm sure of it.'

'I know Howard can't go,' Gavin said. 'He's going away for the weekend. He's joining his wife at her godmother's, he's driving over there this evening, it's all arranged. He mentioned it on the phone yesterday.'

'Then you can ask Mr Roche, I'm sure he'll go. Shall I ring him now?'

'I'd better speak to him myself.' He was beginning to feel a great surge of relief at the prospect of deliverance.

Roche was, as always, ready to be flexible. 'Yes, of course,' he said when the matter had been explained. 'I don't mind in the least.'

'It's very good of you,' Gavin said. 'Particularly at such short notice.'

'It's no trouble. Tomorrow's my turn on duty, I'll stop over here tonight.' Roche and the head clerk at Martleigh took it in turns to go into the office on Saturday mornings.

'I'll get off home then,' Gavin said. 'Thanks again.'

'Look after yourself,' Roche told him. 'There are some pretty nasty bugs going around.'

'Whisky and lemon, that's the thing,' Gavin said. 'I'll stop by for another bottle on the way home, I finished every drop in the house last night.'

'Don't worry about Mr Howard,' Miss Tapsell said

when Gavin had replaced the receiver. 'I'll ring him, I'll explain about the meeting.' She was already shepherding Gavin towards the door. 'I'll see to everything here, don't worry about any of it.' She looked up at him. 'Would you like me to get someone to run you home? Are you sure you feel like driving?'

'Oh, I'll be all right, thanks,' he said. 'I'm quite capable of getting home. I'll sweat it out over the weekend, I'll be as right as rain on Monday.'

With the extra time at his disposal because of the cancelled meeting, Roche was able to get through a good deal of work during the afternoon. At a quarter to five his secretary came in with a pile of letters to be signed. He came suddenly out of his absorption.

'Good heavens,' he said. 'Is that the time?' He reached for the phone. 'I must ring my wife and tell her I won't be home this evening. I meant to do it earlier.'

On Monday morning Mrs Cutler returned to work at Eastwood. She didn't yet feel one hundred per cent her old sprightly self but she felt just about well enough, and it did you no good to stay moping round the house once you were anything at all like fit to get back to work.

She pulled on a thick knitted cap and wound a long woolly scarf round her neck and shoulders, securing it with a large safety-pin against unwinding while she was pedalling along. She was early, as usual on a Monday morning. She always liked to get the week off to a good start, particularly so today, when she hadn't been into Eastwood to clean since last Tuesday. The house would be in a fine old state by now. Mr Elliott was the last person to think of picking up a duster or running the cleaner over a carpet, let alone applying a flick of polish anywhere, not even if she were to stay away weeks instead of days. Not that she thought any the less of him for that.

There was man's work and there was woman's work, and she had never seen good reason to depart from that principle.

She hoisted herself up on to her antiquated bicycle and began to pedal along at a good steady pace. The weekend had been dry, very bright and cold, but this morning was dark and overcast, with a biting wind. Not a morning to tempt folk out unnecessarily. She met no one as she covered the three-quarters of a mile, only a car or two drove past her on its way to Cannonbridge.

She reached Eastwood and got stiffly down to open the gate. She kept her head lowered against the chill blast as she pushed the bicycle along the drive and round to the rear of the house. She stowed the bike away in its usual place inside the shed and went over to the back door. She turned the handle but the door refused to yield. She tried again, without result. Mr Elliott must have forgotten to unlock it for her. He probably hadn't expected her back so soon, it would be a nice surprise for him. She put a finger on the bell and pressed it, glancing about the garden as she waited. A few yards away a fly-catcher darted about, gathering material for his minuscule nest. In a nearby flowerbed a robin tugged at a worm.

Still no sound from inside the house. She pressed the bell again. 'Oh, come on!' she said aloud. 'Get a move on!' She began to stamp her feet to keep the circulation going. Still no sign of Mr Elliott coming down. She abandoned restraint, she put her finger forcefully on the bell and kept it there for several seconds. It was certainly ringing, she could hear it clearly, loud and insistent, he must surely hear it too, wherever he was — but maybe not if he was in the bathroom with the door closed. Or he could have overslept, he might have taken a drink or two over the odds last night, he might still be in bed. She stuck her finger on the bell yet again. She was growing tired of standing out here in the cold.

And then a thought struck her. Maybe he wasn't in the house at all, maybe he'd already gone off to work. He could have had a specially busy day ahead, he could have decided he'd make an early start, he might even have had to go somewhere out of town—he did sometimes have to do that. He wasn't to know she'd be returning to work this morning, he didn't have second sight. She gave a loud noisy sigh at the thought, for it meant she would have had a wasted journey, she'd have to cycle back home again with nothing accomplished, in a bad mood for the rest of the day.

She made a determined movement of her head. She would soon see if her guess was right. She walked across to the garage to find out if his car was gone. The upper sections of the garage doors were glazed. She pressed her forehead against the glass and peered in. The car was there—so he must still be in the house.

She turned away from the garage, frowning. A feeling of bafflement, a stir of disquiet, rose inside her. She stood for a moment thinking what to do next. It wasn't very likely that any of the other doors to Eastwood would be open but she might as well try them, just in case.

There were three other doors to the house, two side doors and the front door. She walked round the back to the side door that faced towards Manor Cottage but she had no luck there. Then she tried the front door, again without success. She stepped back and surveyed the house. The downstairs curtains were drawn back, and the upstairs curtains too—except for the main bedroom, Mr Elliott's bedroom; those were still closed.

But if he was still in the house why didn't he answer her ring? A horrible feeling began to build up inside her head, her heart began to bump and lurch.

She went unsteadily round the side of the house towards the last remaining door. She tried the handle, though now without any hope that it would yield. Then she turned her head and her gaze fell on a window to the left of the door, a little further along; a kitchen window. She stood arrested, staring at it. It was a casement window composed of a number of small panes, and was normally secured from the inside by a lever-type handle. One of the panes had been neatly removed so that it was now possible for a hand to be slipped inside and the lever operated.

Her heart pounded violently, she began to feel very unwell. She went close up to the window and peered into the kitchen; it seemed much as usual. She stood staring in, trying to decide what to do, then she suddenly turned and set off down the drive towards Manor Cottage.

She was out of breath by the time she reached the front door. She stood for a moment with her head lowered and her hand pressed to her side, trying to recover herself before raising the knocker. Before she had time to get her breath back the door swung suddenly open to reveal Emily Picton gazing out at her with sharp interest.

'Is your father in?' Mrs Cutler managed to say.

'Yes.' Emily maintained her unsmiling stare.

'Would you fetch him?' Mrs Cutler said. She was getting her breath back now, thank heavens.

Emily didn't move. 'Why do you want him?' she asked.

Mrs Cutler felt like giving her a good slap. 'If you would just fetch your father,' she said. Too clever by half, that young lady, so sharp she'd cut herself one of these days, and that certainly wouldn't grieve Mrs Cutler.

'What is it, dear?' The voice of Mrs Picton floated into the hall from the direction of the kitchen. Emily all but closed the front door, then she turned and ran back along the passage. The rude little madam, Mrs Cutler thought with heat. She slid the door a little further open and put her ear against the aperture. She could hear a low-pitched exchange of voices and then the sound of Emily running up the stairs, followed by a pause, and then

Emily and her father coming down.

At last the door was thrown open and Mr Picton was standing on the threshold with Emily beside him. 'You needn't concern yourself with this,' he said sharply to Emily and she took herself reluctantly off. 'I'm sorry,' he said to Mrs Cutler. 'Is there something I can do for you?' She began telling him in a garbled rush—for she suddenly felt shaky and tearful—about the window, the curtains, the car, how she couldn't get in, couldn't make Mr Elliott answer.

'I'd better come along and see,' he said as soon as he got the gist of it. 'Just hang on a moment.' He vanished inside and came hurrying back again a few moments later. 'Don't agitate yourself,' he said as they went off together down the path to the gate. 'There's probably some perfectly simple explanation.'

She couldn't keep up with his pace. 'You'd better go on and leave me,' she said after a minute or two. 'I'll follow on.' He gave a nod and set off at a run. He flung open the gate of Eastwood and ran up the drive.

As she followed him through the gate she heard a sound from the cottage. She glanced over and saw the lower sash of a bedroom window being raised, a window overlooking the Eastwood drive. Emily put her head out and gave her a level, unabashed stare, then she turned her head and craned out after her father's speeding figure.

Mrs Cutler followed Mr Picton as quickly as she could but she had to keep stopping to relieve an unpleasant feeling of tightness across her chest. She saw Mr Picton go round the side of the house towards the broken window. As she reached the house the front door opened and Mr Picton stood on the step. He was very pale.

'What is it?' she cried.

He gave her a long look. 'I'm afraid it's pretty bad.'

'What is it?' she cried again. 'What's happened?'

He drew a long breath. 'He's in the house, upstairs. I'm afraid he's dead.'

She gave a sharp cry and put a hand up to her head. Then all at once she made a rush at the steps, pushing past him into the house.

He clutched at her arm. 'Don't go up,' he said urgently. But she shook off his grasp and made for the stairs. 'Don't touch anything!' he called after her. 'I'm phoning the police.' She turned along the landing towards the front bedroom. Downstairs in the hall she could hear Mr Picton dialling.

The bedroom door was open and the lights were on. She stood on the threshold, staring in, looking across at the bed. She felt as if at any moment she would faint clean away but she forced herself to stand there and look. Downstairs she could hear Mr Picton's voice, rapid and urgent.

The bedclothes had been pulled back and something had been thrown down across them, a dark coat or raincoat; that too had been thrown back.

Mr Elliott lay on his right side, facing away from her, his head bent down towards his chest, his left arm over his face, the hand resting on the pillow. She could see the back of his head, the thick dark hair.

The jacket of his pyjamas had been raised, exposing his back. Sticking out from between his shoulder-blades was the long handle of a knife.

CHAPTER 4

In the front bedroom at Eastwood Detective Chief Inspector Kelsey stood with his back to the window, looking across at the bed. He was a big, solidly-built man with a freckled face and shrewd green eyes, and a head of thickly-springing carroty hair.

The photographer had gone. The doctor had finished his examination and gone back to Cannonbridge. The body lay with its face decently covered, waiting to be removed to the mortuary. Throughout the house the long and tedious search for fingerprints was under way, the scrutiny of the garden and surrounding area had begun; a door-to-door inquiry would shortly start in the village.

Kelsey passed a hand across his craggy features. One single blow to the heart, a sure and confident thrust by someone standing over Elliott.

The bedroom was very warm, much warmer than usual, according to Mrs Cutler; Elliott had probably turned up the central heating when he came in, shivering, running a temperature. And also according to Mrs Cutler, he had piled extra blankets on the bed.

By the time the police arrived at Eastwood Mrs Cutler had recovered to some extent from her initial shock. She had helped herself while waiting for the police to a couple of stiff brandies from the drinks cupboard in the dining-room and was in a voluble and flushed state when Kelsey first spoke to her, alternating between bouts of tearfulness and shrewd, sharp-eyed observation.

'Mr Elliott took two extra blankets from the linen chest in the second bedroom,' she had told the Chief. She took him across the landing and showed him an oak chest with the lid thrown back, more blankets folded inside. 'He didn't bother to close the chest,' she said. 'He must have been feeling rotten.' She had begun to sniff again; she took out her handkerchief and dabbed at her eyes.

Either the heat had after a while proved too much for Elliott and he had flung aside the bedclothes as he slept, or else his assailant had drawn aside the covers in order to raise the pyjama jacket and plunge in the knife. Leonard Picton had told them that when he entered the bedroom, the head and upper part of the body had been completely covered by the raincoat; he had also switched on the lights, he had found the room in total darkness. There was no sign of any struggle. It seemed very likely that Elliott had been deeply asleep when he was struck.

'Difficult to say how long he's been dead,' the doctor had said. 'The central heating, the extra bedclothes—it could have been any time in the twelve hours between, say, seven o'clock on Friday evening and seven on Saturday morning.'

Kelsey had asked Mrs Cutler about the raincoat. Had she ever seen it before? Did it belong to Mr Elliott? But she couldn't be sure.

When the body had been removed Kelsey went in search of Mrs Cutler again. She had told them that a number of articles were missing from the house; various pieces of porcelain and glass taken from the open display shelves in the sitting-room. He ran her to earth in the dining-room where she sat at the table with her head lowered and her eyes closed, her hands linked in front of her on the polished top of the table. Leonard Picton was also in the room. He was standing by the window, staring out, his hands clasped behind his back.

Picton had earlier told Kelsey that neither he nor his wife had heard anything untoward from Eastwood during the evening or night of last Friday. They had gone to bed as usual around half past ten, hadn't been awakened during the night by any unusual sounds. Neither of the Pictons had been able to offer any assistance about the raincoat or the knife. They had also said they had never seen or heard anything suspicious, no one hanging round the property, either recently or at any time during the eighteen months they had lived at Manor Cottage; nor had Elliott ever mentioned anything like that to them.

Picton turned now from the window and looked at the Chief with inquiry.

'I think you'd better ring the college and tell them you

won't be in this morning,' Kelsey said in answer to that look. 'Something might crop up, we might want you. But there's no need for you to stay here, you can get off next door. We'll contact you if we need you.'

When he had gone Kelsey sat down opposite Mrs Cutler. 'You've had a chance to look round further,' he said. 'Have you spotted anything else missing?'

She shook her head. 'Not as far as I can see. But I've been thinking about that raincoat. There's a wardrobe in the rear hall, there are some coats hanging up in it. I hardly ever go to that wardrobe but I think perhaps I might have seen a raincoat in there.'

Kelsey got to his feet. 'We'll take a look,' he said.

The rear hall was a fair size with various doors opening out of it. Against one wall stood a mahogany wardrobe. Inside was a rail with several garments on hangers. An old tweed jacket, a fawn trench coat, a waistcoat of quilted nylon, a dark blue anorak. On the floor of the wardrobe was a pair of wellingtons, some black laced shoes, brown leather slip-ons. A shelf above the garments held a grey tweed hat and a pair of string-backed gloves.

'Did Mr Elliott do any gardening himself?' Kelsey asked.

'No, he left all that to Jessup. Jessup comes here three full days a week.'

'Can you say positively if the raincoat came from this wardrobe?'

She screwed up her face, staring in at the garments, then she reluctantly shook her head. 'I'm sorry, I just can't say.' She put a hand up to her face. 'It seems to me now I might have seen it hanging up at the back of the kitchen door.' She shook her head again. 'But there again, I can't be sure.'

'Don't worry about it,' Kelsey said. 'You've been a great help to us.' He closed the wardrobe door. As far as size went, the raincoat could certainly have belonged to the dead man. An ordinary enough garment, quite good quality, nothing special; charcoal grey, a straight un-belted style with raglan shoulders, a dark green plaid lining, a manufacturer's label inside the front lap, a well-known make.

He stood rubbing his big fleshy nose. It was possible that Elliott had still felt cold after he'd gone back to bed with the extra blankets. He couldn't be bothered to go into the other bedroom again, he just got out of bed and snatched up the raincoat—the first coat he laid hands on—from the wardrobe or the back of the door. He threw it down on the bed and jumped back under the covers.

He was probably pretty woozy by that time. A bottle of whisky, half empty, stood on the bedside table. Beside it was a beaker and a bottle of lemon juice, one-third full. An electric kettle stood on a metal tray on the floor by the bed.

Elliott's wristwatch, his keys and wallet, were in a small drawer of the dressing-table; they appeared undisturbed. The intruder—assuming for the moment that it was a burglar—could have approached the bedside table, looking for these things. Elliott could have stirred or groaned in his sleep, could have muttered something; the intruder might have struck out at him in panic, thinking he was waking up.

Mrs Cutler wasn't able to be much more definite about the knife. She thought it was a ham knife but she couldn't say with any certainty if it belonged to the house. It could be one of the knives from the kitchen drawer. She took the Chief into the kitchen and opened the cutlery drawer. Inside were various knives, none of them very new-looking, some with blades worn from long use and much sharpening over the years.

'Nearly all the stuff here at Eastwood came from his father's house,' she said. 'There's some more cutlery in the sideboard in the dining-room. That's better quality, it doesn't get used very often, Mr Elliott didn't do any entertaining here.' She rarely had occasion to look into the sideboard drawer and had only the vaguest idea about what might be in it. She certainly wouldn't expect to be able to identify any particular piece.

Kelsey followed her into the dining-room and looked in the drawer. Everything neatly arranged, of good quality, keen and serviceable. Two of the knives, a breadknife and carving knife, were of a design closely resembling the knife that had killed Elliott, but there was nothing uncommon about the pattern, half the houses in Cannonbridge probably had similar knives.

But Mrs Cutler had no doubts about the murderer. A burglar, of course. 'I told Mr Elliott he was chancing it,' she said, 'keeping all that valuable stuff out on show. The lady at one place where I used to work, she kept everything locked away, she said it was asking for trouble, keeping it out. But Mr Elliott just laughed when I told him.' She looked up at the Chief with a faintly bleary eye. 'He said life was too short to worry about burglars.' She suddenly began to cry, loudly and without restraint. Kelsey made no attempt to stop her. At last her shoulders grew still and she began to draw long sighing breaths; she took out a handkerchief and dabbed fiercely at her eyes and cheeks.

'I think you'd better make some good strong coffee,' Kelsey suggested.

'Yes, I will,' she said at once. 'If you don't mind condensed milk. I always keep a tin in the fridge for myself. Mr Elliott drank his coffee black.' She seemed glad of a reason for more normal activity and went bustling off to the kitchen with Kelsey following.

While she busied herself he stood reading through the list of missing articles she had dictated. So far the search had failed to discover any trace of them in the house or grounds. She had been able to give a detailed description of each piece. 'I've dusted them often enough,' she said. 'If I can't describe them, nobody can.' Birds and animals, figurines and groups, Derby, Meissen, Royal Worcester; some Coalport vases, Nailsea and Bristol glass. 'Mr Elliott knew I appreciated his things,' she said. 'He told me what they were, more than once. It was all family stuff, it came to him from his mother.' Worth a bob or two, Kelsey pondered.

By no means all the objets d'art on show had been taken, about two-thirds still remained. What had gone appeared to be about as much as could be fitted, say, into a sack, no more than a man might comfortably manage on his own; Kelsey had seen no sign that the crime had been the work of more than one intruder.

As Mrs Cutler reached down beakers from an open drawer, the phone rang in the hall. Cannonbridge station again, Kelsey thought; he remained where he was. In the hall a constable lifted the receiver and a minute or two later came looking for the Chief. 'It's a Miss Tapsell,' he said. 'Mr Elliott's secretary. She's ringing from the Cannonbridge office to see why Mr Elliott hasn't come in to work. She sounds very anxious.'

'What did you tell her?' Kelsey asked.

'Nothing. I just asked her to hang on for a moment.'

Kelsey went along to the hall. He never liked breaking news of this kind over the phone; every sort of consideration was against it. But there was no escaping it now. He picked up the receiver.

Miss Tapsell began to speak at once, firing a rapid string of questions, her voice high and brittle with anxiety.

Kelsey declared his identity and allowed a moment or two to pass so that she might begin to grasp the gravity of what she was about to hear before he told her that Elliott was dead.

She found it difficult to take in; she was deeply

shocked, appalled. Then for another minute or two she was clearly under the impression that Elliott had died as a result of the feverish cold that had sent him home early on Friday. Kelsey began gently to disabuse her of the idea. He didn't go into details of the crime but indicated that there appeared to have been a break-in and that Elliott had met a violent end. After a few moments of horrified silence she said in a high, incredulous tone, 'You can't mean he's been murdered?'

'I'm afraid so,' Kelsey said. She began to cry, harshly and jerkily.

'We'll be along to the Cannonbridge office as soon as we can get away from here,' Kelsey told her. 'It'll be some time a little later on this morning. You'd better say something to the staff. We'll have to talk to everyone.'

She stopped crying. 'Mr Elliott's brother,' she said. 'Mr Howard Elliott, over at the Wychford branch, does he know what's happened?'

'Not yet.' Kelsey intended to get over to Wychford as soon as possible to break the news to the brother—or, more accurately, the half-brother—in person.

'He'll be ringing through here,' Miss Tapsell said with dismay. 'He phones this office a lot. I'm surprised he hasn't been on already this morning.' Her voice rose, shrill with anxiety. 'What shall I tell him?'

Kelsey accepted at once that he wouldn't now be able to leave it till he got to Wychford. A great pity, but it couldn't be helped. 'Don't worry,' he said. 'I'll tell him myself. I'll ring him now.' He had never had any dealings with Howard Elliott, had never even spoken to him, but he had seen him years ago with his father at various functions, when Howard had worked at the Cannonbridge office. He remembered him as a quiet, unobtrusive young man, standing very much in his father's shadow.

He put through the call right away. Howard was in his office, dealing with the morning post. Again Kelsey had

to go through the tricky business of breaking the news by
degrees while at the same time trying to assess reactions, a
tone of voice.

There was certainly nothing dramatic about Howard's
response, no horrified exclamations, no rapid outflow of
shocked questions. 'Dead?' he echoed in a tone of
detached incredulity. 'How did he die?' Kelsey answered
his questions, which were brief and matter-of-fact, on the
same lines as he had answered Miss Tapsell.

Howard said he would leave at once for Eastwood but
Kelsey told him there was nothing to be gained by that. 'If
you stay where you are,' he said, 'we'll be with you later
on this morning, after we've been into the Cannonbridge
office. It could be around midday.'

'I don't know if you're aware,' Howard said in an impersonal tone as if talking to a client, 'that there's a third
office, over in Martleigh.' No, Kelsey hadn't been aware
of its existence. 'It's a small branch,' Howard added. 'It's
been open a year or so. The manager is away on sick leave
at present; he's been away some weeks now. Stephen
Roche is running the branch until he gets back. He's the
number two over there, he was at the Cannonbridge
branch before he went to Martleigh.'

'Perhaps you'd have a word with Roche yourself on the
phone,' Kelsey said. 'Explain what's happened.' He
couldn't see much chance of getting over to Martleigh
today. 'Tell him we'll be over there some time tomorrow.'

He went back to the kitchen and Mrs Cutler poured his
coffee. He began to drink it, staring ahead in silence.
Howard Elliott was certainly a cool customer, but so was
his father. Kelsey had had some slight acquaintance with
old Matthew Elliott, an impressive-looking man of considerable presence, a fine head and strongly-marked
features, handsome into old age. Kelsey knew something
of the history of the firm, the scandal years ago, the
divorce, the family feud, all eagerly mulled over by the

local gossips. He had seen Matthew's second wife sometimes with her husband; a beautiful woman with a warm,
friendly smile.

'Do you happen to know if Howard is married?' he
asked Mrs Cutler.

'Yes, he is.' She had met his wife. Mrs Elliott had called
in at Eastwood once or twice while Mrs Cutler was
working in the house, to leave a message or return a book.
'She's a very smartly dressed young woman, quite a bit
younger than her husband.'

'What about Gavin Elliott? Did he have any particular
lady friends? Any fiancée?'

She shook her head. 'He never mentioned anyone.'

'But he did have women friends?'

She moved her shoulders. 'I suppose so, a good-looking
young man like that. But he didn't talk to me about
them. I wouldn't have wanted him to, none of my business. I'm not interested in other people's private lives.'

Indeed? Kelsey thought. In his experience cleaning
ladies harboured a more than ordinary degree of interest
in the doings of their employers, and most particularly in
their private lives. He looked reflectively at Mrs Cutler;
she returned his gaze stolidly. 'There'd be a lot less
trouble in the world if we all minded our own business,'
she said with challenge.

'I dare say you're right,' Kelsey said equably. 'You said
Mr Elliott didn't do any entertaining here?'

'That's right. He ate out most of the time. He wasn't
one of these young men that like cooking. He might grill a
chop or boil an egg, but that was about all. If he wanted to
entertain he took people to a restaurant. The Caprice, he
used to mention that.' She didn't know if he'd belonged to
any clubs, she couldn't recollect his ever mentioning any.

'Did he take any part in village life?'

She shook her head with assurance. 'No, not at all.
He'd give a donation if they called round collecting for

the church or the school, he'd buy raffle tickets, anything like that, he was always very pleasant in his manner. But he didn't go to church, or any of the dances or whist-drives. He never bothered with that sort of thing.' She moved her head. 'I'm not a joiner-in myself, only leads to gossip and scandal-mongering, a waste of time all round.'

'Do you know if he was friendly with anyone in the village? Any local family, perhaps?'

'I don't think so, I'm sure I'd have known if he was.'

'Do you know of any particular men friends?'

She pondered, then shook her head. 'I can't say as I do.' She looked up at him with a hint of irritation. 'I wouldn't expect to know that sort of thing, I came here to clean. Most of the time I was here Mr Elliott was out at work, we didn't stand round chatting.'

'No, of course not,' Kelsey said amiably. 'But some-times a remark gets passed, there's a letter or a phone call, something is said, quite casually.' She made no response but stood waiting for his next question. 'Do you know if he ever got any letters that seemed to disturb him? Any phone calls? Did he ever mention any kind of trouble? Not just recently but at any time?' Again she shook her head.

She had never seen anyone hanging about the property. Mr Elliott had never mentioned seeing anyone dubious near the place.

Kelsey glanced at his watch. Better collect Sergeant Lambert and get off to Cannonbridge, after he'd had another word with the officer supervising the search. He went out through the kitchen door into the garden. The wind had slackened but the sky was still clouded over.

With the officer beside him he glanced over the little pile of objects that had so far been assembled. Nothing that seemed of particular interest: the usual miscellany of potsherds, bits of rubbish blown in from the road, pieces of old gardening tools, that might be expected in any sizable rural garden.

He found Detective-Sergeant Lambert standing by the side door, looking at the broken window which had been neatly and cleanly cut. 'You can fetch the car up,' Kelsey said. 'I'll just have a word with Mrs Cutler, then she can get off home.'

She was still in the kitchen, putting away the coffee things. 'No need for you to stay any longer,' he told her. 'If we need you we'll call in at your cottage.'

She glanced uncertainly about. 'I don't suppose I'll be coming back here any more.' She looked as if she might burst into tears again. 'I'd better collect my bits and pieces.'

'I should take it easy for a day or two,' Kelsey said. 'You could get a bad reaction. See your doctor if you think it's at all necessary. You've had a very nasty shock, it's bound to take it out of you. I should get to bed early tonight, get a good night's sleep.'

'Little did I think,' she said, 'when I got on my bike this morning—' She drew a series of little sniffling breaths. 'If Mr Picton hadn't been there, I don't know what I'd have done.' She looked up at Kelsey. 'He was ever so good about it all, ever so kind, considering.'

There was a tiny pause. 'Considering what?' Kelsey said gently.

She moved a hand. 'Him and Mr Elliott. That row they had.'

There was another little pause. 'What row was that?' Kelsey said in the same soft tone.

CHAPTER 5

'I don't know all the ins and outs of it,' Mrs Cutler said. 'It was one morning just after Mr Elliott had left the house. I was shaking my dusters outside. Mr Picton was down by the gate, I couldn't help hearing what he was shouting—'

'Shouting?'

'Yes, quite loudly.'

'What was he shouting about?'

'Money, investments, the kind of business Mr Elliott's firm does, finance and all that. I got the impression Mr Picton had asked Mr Elliott about investing some money and it hadn't done well.'

'When would this be?'

'A week or two back.'

No, Mr Elliott hadn't seemed upset by the episode, he didn't argue with Picton or shout back, he just seemed to be trying to ignore him. No, he hadn't said anything about it to her afterwards.

Kelsey frowned as he came out of the house. He looked up and saw Sergeant Lambert who had brought the car up to the front door. 'We can't get off just yet,' Kelsey told him. 'We'll pop over to Manor Cottage first. I want another word with Picton.' As they walked down the drive he repeated the gist of what Mrs Cutler had just told him.

Picton had certainly said that he and his family were not on close terms with Elliott but he had definitely given the impression of ordinary friendly neighbourliness. He had implied that it suited both parties to preserve a certain distance between the households; they all liked their privacy.

He had also said that neither he nor his wife had seen Elliott for some days, but that this was in no way unusual.

Picton added that his daughter Emily had spoken to Elliott on Friday. Kelsey had then talked to Emily in Picton's presence; she had point blank refused to go off to school at the usual time, consumed with curiosity about what was going on at Eastwood.

Emily told the Chief that after she finished her dinner on Friday she went out into the garden for a few minutes before cycling back to school. That would be about a quarter to one. She saw Elliott drive up in his car. He looked flushed and ill, he had a violent fit of sneezing when he got out to open the gate. She went up to him and asked if he was all right. 'He said he felt terrible,' Emily said with relish. 'I told him we always take elderflower for colds and 'flu, and he said, Well I don't, I take whisky and plenty of it. He said he was going to make himself a hot toddy and go straight to bed, then he got back into his car. I told him I'd close the gate after him.' He had driven up to the house and she had gone off to school. She had seen no one hanging round the property.

When they reached the Eastwood gate Kelsey halted. He turned and surveyed both properties. Manor Cottage was a two-storeyed dwelling set close down by the road, Eastwood stood some fifteen yards farther back; there were no other dwellings within a quarter of a mile.

On the side of the cottage facing towards Eastwood there were two windows on each floor. The farther of the upper windows was of frosted glass, most probably a bathroom window; the nearer window should give a clear view of a good part of the Eastwood house and grounds.

They walked up the path to the front door of the cottage and Lambert gave a brisk rat-tat. A minute or two later Mrs Picton came to the door. Lambert ran his eye over her. She wouldn't be half so plain if she took just a little care over her appearance, if she abandoned her Victorian-governess hairstyle for something softer, added a touch of colour to the general monotone with a little make-up. Her present appearance was in no way improved by a large, raw and painful-looking cold sore at the side of her mouth.

'My husband's down the garden,' she told them. 'I'll tell him you're here.'

'No need to disturb him,' Kelsey said. 'We'll take a walk down the garden and have a word with him shortly. I think you might be able to help us. We're drawing up a map of the area, roads, dwellings and so on. I wonder if you'd allow us to take a look round the cottage—the general situation with regard to Eastwood, the lay-out of the rooms and so on.'

'Yes, of course, whatever you need to do, go right ahead.' She stepped aside for them to enter. There was a sudden loud whooshing sound from the kitchen and she gave a startled cry.

'My beans!' She darted back along the passage. A highly disagreeable odour of bean-water sizzling on the hotplate penetrated the hall. Kelsey wrinkled his nose as he walked along the passage to the kitchen. Mrs Picton was dabbing at the cooker with a cloth that gave off a cloud of steam.

In marked contrast to Eastwood where scarcely a morsel of food was to be found in the entire house, the kitchen here seemed to be overflowing with food in various stages of preparation. Basins stood ranged along a side table, filled with pulses and dried fruits soaking in water. In the middle of a large table in the centre of the room was a mound of freshly scrubbed vegetables.

'I can see you're up to your eyes in it,' Kelsey said. 'We won't keep you from your work. We'll have a little nip round, upstairs and down, if that's all right with you.'

'Oh—yes, if you don't mind,' she said with relief. She crossed to the sink and wrung out her cloth. There was no sign of Emily. Presumably she'd at last been persuaded to mount her bicycle and pedal off to school.

'We won't be many minutes,' Kelsey said. 'Just forget we're here.' He was already in the passage, opening doors, glancing in, swiftly assessing, his eyes roving at great speed round the interiors.

From neither of the ground-floor windows on the Eastwood side could anything be glimpsed of the neighbouring house or garden. In each room in turn Kelsey glanced rapidly over shelves and into cabinets, he opened cupboards and cast a swift eye over the contents, giving a second look at any ornaments. There were very few, and none of any value.

One of the two upstairs rooms on the Eastwood side was indeed a bathroom. A transom light stood open but it afforded no view worth mentioning. He tried the window but it showed no inclination to budge. He abandoned his effort and went along to the room next door. This was clearly Emily's bedroom, furnished with a pretty chintz. There were two windows here, one overlooking the front garden and road, and a side window overlooking Eastwood; it was open a few inches at the top. He tried raising the lower sash; it rose smoothly under his fingers. He leaned out. He was looking over the Picton's boundary wall; he had a wide, clear view of the front garden next door, the front and side of the house.

Of the two remaining rooms on the other side of the landing, the front one was the main bedroom, with twin beds, and the second room had been fitted up as a study. In all four rooms he glanced over shelves and into cupboards but came across nothing of significance.

When they came downstairs again they found Mrs Picton chopping vegetables at great speed. She offered to make them a hot drink but Kelsey declined. 'Thanks for your help,' he said. 'We won't bother you any further. We'll step outside now and have a word with your husband.'

Picton was digging a trench in the vegetable plot. He

turned his head at the sound of their approach.

'One or two little additional points that have come up,' Kelsey said. Picton said nothing. He stood leaning on his spade, waiting for the Chief to continue. 'You gave me to understand,' Kelsey said in the same tone of pleasant neutrality, 'that you were on ordinary neighbourly terms with Gavin Elliott.' Picton inclined his head. 'Do you stand by that?'

'Yes, of course,' Picton said on a note of surprise.

'There was never any disagreement between you?'

Picton moved his shoulders. 'Nothing of any consequence.'

'Then there was some minor disagreement?'

Picton jerked his head. 'You're bound to get some disagreements between neighbours.'

'Could you be more specific?' Kelsey persisted.

'We had a trifling argument about the money market,' Picton said. 'Elliott was by way of considering himself an expert on such matters. I didn't altogether agree with some of his views.'

'That's all there was to it? Opinions about the state of the stock market?'

'That kind of thing,' Picton said lightly. 'Nothing to get steamed up about.'

'Nothing to shout about?' Kelsey said. 'Nothing to stand in the Eastwood driveway and shout about?'

'What gives you that impression?' Picton asked with an air of mild amusement.

There was no answering amusement in the Chief's green eyes. 'Did you on any occasion stand in the Eastwood drive and shout at Elliott in consequences of some argument about stocks and shares?'

'I don't know that I'd use the word shout,' Picton said with a detached, considering air. 'I may have got a trifle heated. It certainly didn't bother Elliott, he was more amused than anything. He thought me a tyro in such matters, a bit of a rural hick. He didn't take my views very seriously.'

'Did you ever ask his advice about investments?'

'We did have one or two chats about investment. He told me he liked certain shares, nothing more than that.'

'Did you ever invest money on the strength of these casual chats?'

'I may have been influenced to some extent by what he said.'

'And were you later dissatisfied with the performance of your purchases?'

Picton smiled. 'They're long-term investments. I didn't buy for a quick profit. I'll decide in four or five years if I'm satisfied or not.'

'Did you ever complain to Elliott about the poor performance of your investments?'

'No, I did not. As I said, we merely had different opinions about how the market might react to a given situation.' He gazed blandly at the Chief.

Kelsey changed tack abruptly. 'Where were you living before you moved to Manor Cottage?'

Picton tilted back his head. 'Over in Ellenborough.' This was a large town some forty-five miles away.

'Were you teaching in Ellenborough?'

Picton gave a nod. 'I was at the College of Further Education.' Ellenborough was twice the size of Cannonbridge; the Ellenborough college was large and old-established, with a very sound reputation.

'Why did you apply for a job at the Cannonbridge college?' Kelsey asked. 'It can scarcely have been promotion.'

Picton waved a hand. 'I'm not a man to chase after every penny, I'm a good deal more interested in the quality of life. We fancied a more rural existence.'

'You could have found a cottage outside Ellenborough. You could have stayed in the same job.'

'I'd got tired of working in a large town. I wanted less

pressure, less rush and bustle.' He grinned. 'Middle age coming on, I dare say. One loses the appetite for noise and crowds.'

'How long were you in Ellenborough?'

'Long enough. A few years.' I'll get over to Ellenborough pretty smartly, Kelsey thought; see what they've got to say about him over there.

'Your wife's been kind enough to let us look over the cottage,' he said. 'We're making a map of the area, the lay-out of buildings, roads, footpaths, and so on. I take it you've no objection to my men going over your garden, looking into sheds and outhouses?'

'No objection at all. They can go anywhere they want. Will it be all right if I go in to work this afternoon?'

'Yes, you can get off.'

Picton drove his spade into the earth with energy. 'If any more little details arise,' he said with a half-smiling air, 'you know where to find me.'

An air of shock brooded over the Cannonbridge office of Elliott Gilmore, there were subdued voices, unsmiling glances, an absence of the usual orderly bustle. The chief clerk, Armitage, was on the look-out for them and appeared in the reception hall as soon as they came in through the front door. He was a man of fifty or so, and had worked for the firm all his life; he was accustomed to acting as manager whenever the necessity arose. He was short and slightly built, with a deeply lined face and an air of quiet competence. Miss Tapsell hovered a few feet behind Armitage, her face pale and her eyes puffy. Armitage showed the two men into his office and Miss Tapsell followed them inside.

Kelsey disclosed the bare facts of Gavin Elliott's death but he neither offered nor encouraged speculation or deductions from the facts. 'I'll speak to all the staff together,' he said, 'and then briefly to everyone individually. There won't be time for anything more today. We'll be back again first thing in the morning.'

He showed them the raincoat in its protective plastic wrapping and asked if either of them recognized the garment. Armitage shook his head but Miss Tapsell leaned forward and studied the coat with frowning concentration. It had been folded with part of the front lap turned back to expose the plaid lining and the manufacturer's label.

'I believe I have seen it before,' she said. 'I think it used to hang in the broom cupboard—where Mrs Worrall keeps her cleaning things.' She looked up at the Chief. 'I think it belonged to Mr Gavin.'

Kelsey asked her to show him the broom cupboard and she took him down to a cubbyhole in the basement. Inside was a vacuum cleaner, an assortment of mops, brushes and dusters, tins of polish, cans of air freshener. A row of hooks on the wall held a nylon overall and a rayon headscarf, but no raincoat.

'I'm pretty sure it used to hang here,' Miss Tapsell said with a note of growing conviction. 'I remember coming down here once or twice to speak to Mrs Worrall when she was going off in the morning, putting away her cleaning things. I'm sure I saw a grey raincoat hanging up.'

'When was the last time you remember seeing it?'

She bit her lip. 'I'm afraid I can't be exact. It was some time ago.'

'Days? Weeks? Months?'

She stared at the hooks. 'Weeks or months, certainly not days.' She shook her head. 'I'm sorry I can't be more precise.'

Armitage assembled the staff—some dozen of them—in the general office. Two members of staff were away, a woman clerk close to retirement, at home with bronchial trouble after a heavy cold, and a male bookkeeper on holiday with his wife in the United States; they had been there for a fortnight and were due to return in another week.

Kelsey ranged his eyes over them. A silent, tense bunch, every face to some extent wary and guarded against what he might be going to tell them. He spoke in a quiet, informal fashion, but at the mention of the manner of Elliott's death a spasm of horror rippled across the faces before him. One of the women put a hand over her eyes and another began to sob silently.

He produced the raincoat but no one recognized the garment. He asked if any of them had had occasion to go down to the cleaning cupboard in the basement but there was a general shaking of heads.

He then spoke briefly to each of them in a side office. No one had any information or speculation to offer; no one had had any personal association with Elliott outside business hours. No one knew of any disagreement or other circumstance likely to provoke violent reaction among Elliott's clients, colleagues or business associates.

Kelsey then talked again at greater length to Armitage and Miss Tapsell. He saw Armitage first. He answered all the Chief's questions readily and in a straightforward manner. As far as he knew there was no trouble with any account; the firm was in no kind of financial difficulty; there had been no disagreement with Mr Howard Elliott or Mr Roche; he knew nothing of Gavin's personal life.

He left the office and Miss Tapsell took his place, facing Kelsey across the desk. She looked calm and con-trolled, her posture easy and relaxed, but Sergeant Lambert, sitting some little distance behind her, to one side, could see her hands clasped together, tightly clenched, on her lap.

Kelsey began by taking her over the same ground, and with the same result. Yes, she had thought Gavin got on well with his half-brother and with Roche. She told him how Roche had gone to the Chamber of Commerce dinner in Northgrove on Friday evening in Gavin's place.

'Why didn't Gavin ask Howard to go?' Kelsey wanted to know.

'He knew Mr Howard couldn't go. He was going away for the weekend straight after work, he was joining his wife.'

'Stephen Roche lives over in Martleigh, I take it?' Kelsey said.

'No, he lives in Cannonbridge. He has a house on the outskirts.' She explained about the roadworks, the traffic delays, Roche's decision to find lodgings in Martleigh during the week. 'I can give you his Martleigh address,' she said. 'I dare say he'll decide to move house if he stays on at the Martleigh office.'

'Is there some doubt about that?' Kelsey asked as she wrote down the address.

'There's been some talk of opening a fourth branch and Mr Roche might be asked to move there.'

No, she had no knowledge of Gavin's private life, or of any close friendships. 'Was there ever any involvement — as far as you know — with any of the female staff here?' Kelsey asked her. Gavin might not have been his father's son for nothing. The Chief had run his eye over the female staff with that thought in mind, but nowhere had he encountered a face that might tempt a man to folly. Only one of the female clerks was under thirty, and she was a sensible-looking girl; she was engaged to a young man in the same branch.

Miss Tapsell hesitated. 'Well?' Kelsey said on a more peremptory note.

'I don't know if there was anything in it. I wouldn't like you to think . . .' Her voice trailed away.

'I won't jump to conclusions,' Kelsey said.

'It was a girl we had working here. She left about fifteen months ago, when she got married.' She moved her head. 'It was just her manner towards Mr Gavin, a look. I came into the room once or twice when they were together. There was—an atmosphere.'

'No more than that?'

'It was just an impression I had.' She gave him a direct look. 'I never got that impression about any of the other women on the staff.'

'And this man she married?'

'She was engaged to him for quite some time and then it was broken off, I don't know why. It was after that that I began to notice this atmosphere between her and Mr Gavin. That would be about eighteen months ago. Then she made it up with her fiancé and they got married soon afterwards.'

'Where is this young woman now? I'd better have her name.'

'Knightly, Sandra Knightly, that's her married name. They live over in Wychford. She works at the Wychford branch of Elliott Gilmore. She transferred there when she got married.'

'Does her husband work for the firm?'

'No, he's the manager of a supermarket in Wychford, a new place, the Eagle, it opened about fifteen months ago. That was why they got married when they did. He got the job and he asked her to make it up. They got married right away.'

'What age is Mrs Knightly?'

'Twenty-four or five now, I should think. Her husband's quite a bit older, a good ten years, I'd say.'

Kelsey glanced at his watch. Time he was getting over to Wychford himself. 'And as far as you know,' he said on a conclusive note, 'Mr Gavin had no worries, no disagreements—' She began to shake her head and then suddenly stopped. She put a hand up to her mouth.

'Yes?' Kelsey gave her a sharp glance.

'I've just remembered. Mr Gavin's neighbour—'

Kelsey sat back in his chair. 'Leonard Picton?'

'Yes, that's the name.' She explained about Picton's investments, his subsequent resentment. 'Mr Gavin mentioned it as a joke at first, he laughed about it. But then one morning, a week or two back, when he came into the office, he said, "Picton'll go round the twist one of these days. It's getting beyond a joke." He wasn't laughing when he said that.'

'Do you know if Picton ever made any kind of threat?'

She turned her head and looked down at the floor. 'One day last week, Tuesday or Wednesday, when Mr Gavin came in, he told me Picton had been standing waiting for him again, down by the gate. He'd done that more than once. He'd started arguing, saying he'd sue the firm and so on. Mr Gavin didn't speak to him, he didn't even look at him, he just got out of the car to open the gate and got straight back in again.'

'And?'

She looked up at the Chief. 'Picton stuck his head in at the car window. He said, "Cut me dead, would you? Two can play at that game! Watch out I don't cut you down to size!" '

CHAPTER 6

The death of Gavin Elliott was already creating a shocked stir in the town of Cannonbridge but over in Wychford, ten miles away, it had caused scarcely a ripple.

The Wychford branch of Elliott Gilmore was housed in a handsome Victorian crescent on a rise overlooking the main shopping area. The atmosphere inside the office was marginally less disjointed than at Cannonbridge; Gavin's death hadn't involved such immediate and direct upheaval, and to several of the staff he had not been at all well known.

Kelsey intended to follow the same pattern here. He would speak briefly to Howard Elliott before talking to the staff, then again to Howard at greater length.

Howard had cancelled his immediate appointments and was waiting for them in his office. He's put on a good deal of weight, Kelsey thought as Howard stood up from his desk; he looks already well into middle age, though he can't be more than—what? Forty-two or -three? But he still had the same calm and settled air, in spite of the morning's tragic news and the disturbance to routine that must have followed.

The Chief introduced Sergeant Lambert who had never before clapped eyes on Howard; he looked at him now with interest. A rather ponderous appearance, and a rather ponderous manner, certainly nothing dashing or debonair about him. Expensive, well-cut dark business suit, a London tailor, if Lambert was any judge: carefully manicured hands, a good haircut. But the complexion was already growing florid, with patches of broken veins on the cheeks and nose, giving him a coarse, weather-beaten look, like a golf professional or a man who had played a lot of rugger in his youth. I'd credit him with a sulky temper, Lambert thought, not quick to anger and then everything forgotten five minutes later, but a slow, brooding temperament.

Howard shook hands and they all sat down; Howard sat waiting for Kelsey to speak. I'd have expected someone in his situation to ask at once exactly how his half-brother died, Lambert thought. Howard looked a controlled, contained man, always waiting for someone else to make the first move.

The Chief indicated his immediate intentions with regard to the Wychford branch and his more general intentions with regard to the firm. 'We'll be putting men in over the next day or two to look at the books and files,' he said. 'In all three offices. It's always done in cases of this nature. We'll try not to cause too much disruption.'

Howard moved his head. 'Yes, of course. Anything any of us can do to help — naturally we're all at your disposal.'

There was a brief silence and then, as Howard still didn't ask any questions, Kelsey told him the bald facts of Gavin's death. Howard looked down at his desk as he listened. When the Chief came to a stop he gave a single nod but made no other response. Perhaps he finds it difficult to express his feelings, Lambert thought, and so he says nothing at all.

'I've spoken to Stephen Roche over the phone,' Howard offered at last.

'We'll be going over to Martleigh sometime tomorrow,' Kelsey said. 'Probably during the morning.' He produced the raincoat and Howard looked at it stolidly, with no sign of emotion; then he shook his head slowly. 'I'm afraid it means nothing to me.'

'You never saw your brother wearing it?'

'No.'

'Did you ever see it hanging up in the broom cupboard in the basement at the Cannonbridge office?'

Howard looked at him in surprise. 'It's a long time since I've set foot in that basement, I've no idea what's down there now.'

'Can you recall seeing the raincoat hanging up behind the kitchen door at Eastwood?' Again Howard shook his head.

'Did you see much of your brother — apart from contacts in the course of business? Did you see much of him socially? On a personal, family basis?'

'A certain amount, not a great deal. We were virtual strangers till a couple of years ago.' He paused. 'I don't know if you're familiar with the circumstances —' He flicked an inquiring glance at Kelsey, who gave a diplomatic nod in reply, to indicate that he was aware of the family history. 'We had him over to dinner from time to time,' Howard said, 'and he took my wife and myself out to dinner at a restaurant occasionally, always with other guests.' After a moment he added, 'He belonged to one or two clubs. I can give you their names.'

'You called in at Eastwood sometimes?' Kelsey said. You and your wife?'

'Yes, occasionally. On the way home from the Caprice, for a nightcap. Or to pick him up if he and I were going to some function together.' Howard's tone lightened fractionally. 'But I certainly wouldn't expect to know what garments he had hanging up at the back of his kitchen door.'

'Do you know if any of the staff here had any social contact with your brother—on a personal level?'

'I certainly never heard of any such contact.' Howard's tone indicated that he would have considered such contact very bad form.

'Right, then.' Kelsey got to his feet. 'I'll see the staff now, then we can have another chat afterwards.'

The Wychford branch was roughly two-thirds the size of the parent branch, with a correspondingly smaller staff; there were no absentees today.

As they filed into the main office where the Chief intended to address them, Lambert ran his eye over them, singling out one girl almost at once. That's Sandra Knightly, he thought, I'm willing to bet. Not that she was spectacularly gorgeous but she was easily the best-looking female in the room. Average height, a good figure, dark auburn hair and a creamy skin. Eyes—when she glanced across and met the sergeant's gaze—of a light clear hazel, large and well set.

Then another woman took Lambert's eye, one of the last to enter and take her seat. Fifty or more but clearly fighting every inch of the way. Still coloured her eyelids and tinted her hair, dressing it in a style ten or fifteen years too young for her; her clothes were too casually youthful. But her legs were still undeniably good, he saw with an appreciative eye. Long, slender, shapely legs, narrow feet in elegant, high-heeled shoes.

He turned his attention to her face. Something spiteful there, faintly malicious. She conducted herself with confidence, glancing about with the settled, proprietary air of an employee of long standing. But while the others bunched in twos and threes, their heads close together like horses in the shafts, whispering, exchanging confidences and reassurances, she sat by herself; no one spoke to her, no one glanced at her.

It didn't seem to bother her. She looked with sharp interest at the Chief who was standing facing them, to one side of the desk. Her gaze wandered over to Lambert and their eyes met. A shrewd, cold regard, assessing and calculating, changing an instant later to a stare of bold appraisal, decidedly laced with flirtation.

There was a slight stir as Kelsey began to speak, then they settled into total stillness. No one recognized the raincoat, no one had anything to offer—in public, at least. And very little more when Kelsey saw them individually. Even the spiteful-looking fifty-year-old responded to the Chief's questions with no more than silent headshakes. Lambert made a particular note of her name—Mrs Dolphin.

He had certainly been right about the auburn-haired girl, she gave her name as Mrs Sandra Knightly. She sat facing Kelsey with an unsmiling look, her face calm and blank, her hands lightly folded on her lap.

'You worked over at the Cannonbridge branch, I believe?' Kelsey said after the routine questions had produced little response.

'Yes, but not recently.' She had a pleasant voice, well modulated, free from spurious gentility. 'I left when I got married, fifteen months ago.'

'Did you have any contact with Gavin Elliott during those fifteen months?' Kelsey asked in a bland, neutral tone. 'Other than in the way of business?'

'No, I didn't.' She sounded surprised.

'You did have some personal association with him when you were working at the Cannonbridge branch?'

She began to twist her hands together. 'It didn't mean anything.'

'Were you on close terms with him at that time?'

She shook her head, with force. 'No. We just had dinner together once or twice, that was all.'

Kelsey regarded her. 'Does your husband know of this—very slight—relationship?'

She looked at him with anxiety. 'No. There's no reason why he should. We weren't engaged at the time—it was after I'd broken off the engagement. I never went out with Gavin when I was engaged to Frank.' Kelsey said nothing. 'I don't want Frank to know about it,' she said in a sharper, higher, tone.

'Why not? If there was nothing in it.'

'He wouldn't understand. He'd think—' She stopped.

'The jealous type, is he?'

She said nothing but sat looking at him in silence. 'You won't tell him?' she said at last.

'I certainly don't go out of my way to go round handing out information. I see my function as trying to gather it.' He gave her a direct look. 'Not always with as much success as I could wish for. I repeat: Were you on close terms with Elliott? Intimate terms?'

She looked as if she would burst into tears, and shook her head in silence.

'Where was your husband last Friday evening?' Kelsey said suddenly.

She gave a little gasp, then she made an effort to take hold of herself. 'He was at a meeting. We were both there. The Ratepayers' Action Group, here in Wychford.

He was one of the speakers.'

'What time was this?'

Her tone was firmer now, more confident. 'The meeting started at half past seven, it finished about a quarter past ten. We took seven or eight people home with us for coffee, they stayed till getting on for midnight.'

'And then?' Kelsey said. 'What did your husband do then?'

She looked baffled. 'He went to bed, of course.'

'You sleep in the same room?'

She was rigid again with tension. 'Yes, of course we do.'

'You'd better nip along to the Eagle Supermarket when we've finished here,' Kelsey said to Lambert when the door had closed behind her. 'Take a look at her husband.' Kelsey would be going with Howard Elliott to identify the body 'And there are one or two other odds and ends you can clear up while you're about it,' Kelsey added. 'The Eastwood gardener, Jessup, and that clerk that's away ill from the Cannonbridge branch, you'd better have a word with both of them.'

Howard received the news that he would have to identify the body with no show of surprise. It seemed there were no other close relatives. 'There are some cousins in Cornwall,' he told the Chief. 'On my father's side. I haven't seen them since I was a child. I doubt if Gavin ever met them.' He knew nothing of any relatives of Gavin's mother, Gavin had never mentioned any.

'We should have the results of the post mortem this evening,' Kelsey said. 'I'll come out to Claremont and tell you—and your wife—the findings. Your wife's back home, I take it? I understand you were both away for the weekend.'

'Yes, we were staying with my wife's godmother, Mrs Fiske.' Kelsey made a note of the name, and Mrs Fiske's address. 'My wife came back with me last night,' Howard added. 'I told her about Gavin over the phone. She was very upset; she couldn't believe it.'

'Was she a close friend of Gavin's?'

'No, not really.' Howard lifted a pen on his desk, let it drop again. 'But it was a terrible shock, all the same.'

Kelsey asked if he knew of any special women friends of Gavin's.

'He wasn't engaged or anything like that,' Howard said. 'There's a girl, Charlotte Neale—the Neales at Berrowhill Court.' Kelsey knew the name, it meant race-horses to him. 'He talked of her once or twice, he seemed rather keen. But it was very early days, they only met recently, and she's very young.'

'Berrowhill Court,' Kelsey said as he made a note.

'She's not there now, she's on holiday in Switzerland. She's been there a week or two. She's not due back just yet.'

Kelsey asked if he knew of any trouble with clients or business associates. Howard shook his head. 'Does the name Picton mean anything to you?' Kelsey said. Howard shook his head again. 'He lives at Manor Cottage,' Kelsey added. 'Next door to Eastwood.'

'Oh—him! I didn't know his name, or if I did I'd for-gotten it. Yes, Gavin did mention some argy-bargy they'd had, but he didn't take it seriously, he thought the fellow was a bit of a nutter.' He stopped abruptly. 'You surely don't think—'

'We don't think anything at this stage. We're just trying to get to know all the facts.'

'Yes, of course. I'm afraid I can't tell you any more about the row with Picton, Gavin just mentioned it in passing.' He blew out a long breath. 'I still can't take it in that he's dead. When I spoke to him on Friday evening—'

'Friday evening?' Kelsey echoed sharply. 'What time was that?'

'Seven, eight, I can't be sure.'

'Where did you phone from?'

Howard shifted in his chair. 'From Claremont, my own house.'

'But I understood you left for the weekend immediately after work.'

'That was the arrangement, but I was tired when I got home, I didn't relish the idea of a couple of hours' driving. I couldn't see any particular reason to get there that evening.' He moved a hand. 'So I rang Judith and told her I wouldn't be leaving till the morning.'

'How did Gavin seem when you rang him?'

'He sounded dopey. He said he'd been asleep, the phone had wakened him. I think he'd drunk a fair amount of hot toddy. I didn't keep him chatting, I just asked if there was anything I could do, anything I could bring over, but he said no, he had all he wanted, he was going to sweat it out over the weekend.'

Kelsey got to his feet. 'Time we were getting over to the mortuary.'

As Sergeant Lambert pushed back his chair a thought suddenly struck him: Howard could have gone to the Northgrove dinner after all.

CHAPTER 7

The Eagle Supermarket stood on the edge of Wychford. One of its chief attractions was a vast car park, nearly empty when Lambert drove into it shortly after lunch—in his case a sandwich and a cup of coffee. The breeze was still cold but a thin sunlight was struggling through as he made his way across the car park.

He went in through the swing doors and picked up a wire basket. It was a bare place with no frills, apparently aiming to entice custom by prices pared to the bone. The tide of shoppers had receded and young men were busy replenishing the shelves against the afternoon wave.

At the end of an aisle Lambert saw an office marked: MANAGER: F. R. KNIGHTLY. A few moments later a man in a business suit approached the door with an air of speed and resolution and went inside. Lambert walked up the aisle. When he had almost reached the top the door opened again and the same man came out. He was frowning, and looked in a sour, irritable mood. He glanced about with a penetrating gaze, raised a hand and called out a name. One of the young men instantly abandoned his shelf-filling and went towards him almost at a run.

Lambert drifted a little nearer, scanning the shelves, picking up tins, examining and replacing them. Knightly appeared to be passing on some complaint from a customer, rebuking and exhorting. He waved a hand, dismissing the youth back to his chore, then stood glancing rapidly about with a critical eye. Lambert began to make his way down the next aisle, all the time keeping his quarry in view.

Knightly set off on a quick jerky tour of the store, with Lambert altering his position from time to time to keep him in sight. Knightly wouldn't have been bad-looking except for his habitual frowning expression and an air of being permanently about to strike, like a cobra. He stopped every few yards, indicating with a stabbing finger some fault or omission. The checkout girls sat bolt upright as soon as he appeared in view, they stopped chattering to each other and began to flash helpful smiles at the customers.

After some minutes of this darting inspection he suddenly turned and went back to his office. He didn't emerge again during the further five minutes Lambert spent wandering about. The tension visibly relaxed, the staff began to smile and joke again between themselves.

There was a sergeant at the Wychford station with whom Lambert had some brief friendly court acquaintance. I'll look in and see if I can get a word with him, he decided, see if he can tell me anything about Knightly.

He was in luck. The sergeant was on duty and at a loose end. 'I don't know Knightly myself,' he told Lambert, 'but old Jock Steen, he knows everyone in Wychford. Come and have a word with him.' Jock Steen was a sergeant in the uniformed branch, now close to retirement. They found him down in the canteen.

'Frank Knightly,' Steen said. 'Yes, I know him.' He stirred his tea. 'His father was a counterhand at a grocer's in the town. Frank always had ambitions.' He jerked his head. 'Looks like he's all set to achieve some of them. He's standing for the local council, spends his spare time knocking on doors, drumming up votes.'

'How does his wife feel about that?' Lambert asked.

Steen eyed him reflectively. Lambert hadn't indicated why he was asking about Knightly. 'She goes along with it,' he said. 'Pretty girl, Sandra Knightly, good photograph of her in last week's *Chronicle*, some charity do she and Frank went to, they're never out of the paper.' He took a drink of his tea. 'What's Frank been up to?'

Lambert gave a half-smiling shake of his head. 'I don't know that he's been up to anything.'

'I could believe Knightly capable of a lot,' Steen said. 'He's ruthless and grasping and self-seeking.' He drained his beaker and set it down with a little clatter. 'But what I couldn't under any circumstances believe is that he would do anything, anything at all, that would in the slightest degree spoil his chances of getting a seat on the council in May.'

The offices of the *Wychford Chronicle* were cramped and old-fashioned, housed in a small decrepit building squeezed into one of the many alleyways in the warren of streets near the centre of the old part of town. Inside the offices there was a good deal of dust about, but it didn't

seem to interfere with efficiency or cheerfulness. A helpful young woman took charge of Lambert, showed him
where he could look through back copies of the paper.

He came across the Knightlys several times in the
course of the last few months, smiling at an old folks'
party, attending a charity concert, a Mayoral reception,
spearing barbecue sausages, organizing local petitions. He
bought enlarged copies of two recent photographs which
gave good clear pictures of Sandra Knightly.

He looked at his watch as he came out of the *Chronicle*
office. He was due to meet the Chief at the Cannonbridge
police station at five-thirty; that should give him time,
after he'd made his other two calls, to pop along to the
Caprice restaurant with his photographs.

The bronchitic lady clerk lived in a small detached house
in a quiet suburb of Cannonbridge. It took Lambert some
minutes to gain admittance. But she must be in, he
thought, resolutely continuing to press the bell at
intervals. At last he heard the sound of movement and a
little later a woman huddled in a thick dressing-gown, her
bare feet thrust into slippers, opened the door a fraction
and peered out at him with an expression that was far
from welcoming. Her face was pale and blotchy, her
greying brown hair was pulled untidily back and secured
on each side with a large hairclip.

'Yes?' she said with an exhausted air.

Lambert introduced himself. He apologized for dis-
turbing her and asked if he might step inside. 'I'm afraid I
have some bad news,' he said. She made a sound of
distress and put a hand up to her face. 'It's nothing to do
with you personally,' he added. 'Nothing to do with any
of your family.' She drew a little trembling breath and
held the door back for him to enter.

The air inside was oppressively hot and smelled
strongly of some medicated vapour rub. He got her to sit

down while he broke the news of Elliott's death; he sat patiently by while she had her cry; he went into the kitchen and made tea for her when she had recovered a little. She sipped at her tea and the colour began to return to her cheeks. 'Poor Mr Elliott,' she said. 'He was such a nice young man. I can't really take it in.'

Lambert showed her the raincoat and asked if she had ever seen it before. She scrutinized it with frowning concentration. 'I'm not sure,' she said hesitantly. She glanced up at him with apology, bent her head and looked at the coat again. She seemed to feel she owed it to him to recognize the garment, that it was the least she could do after he'd taken the trouble to call and tell her about her employer's death.

'Don't worry about it,' Lambert said gently. 'It doesn't matter if you can't recognize it.'

She sat back with an air of relief. 'Oh well, in that case I'm afraid I can't be of any assistance. I'm pretty certain I've never seen it before.' No, she had never been down to the cleaning cupboard in the basement, the occasion had never arisen.

Nor could she tell him anything about Gavin's personal life. She had found him an easy man to work for, courteous and considerate. 'I always felt he was anxious to get on well with people,' she said. 'He was always very insistent on a friendly, pleasant atmosphere in the firm.' She moved her head. 'But that didn't mean he couldn't take decisions, unpopular ones if he had to.'

'You worked for his father before him?' Lambert said.

'Yes, I've always worked at Elliott Gilmore. I thought the world of Mr Matthew, he was a man of great character. I remember the day he brought Mr Gavin into the office for the first time. He was such a fine-looking boy, such an open, cheerful manner.' Tears glittered in her eyes, she took out a handkerchief and dabbed at them. 'Mr Matthew was so proud of him, so fond of him.'

'You'd know Mr Howard Elliott too in those days? When he worked at the main office.'

'Yes, I knew him as a young man, before there was all the trouble about the divorce.' She shook her head. 'Such a tragedy when a family breaks up like that. Mr Howard was well enough in his way, I certainly wouldn't want to criticize him, but he never had the manner, he was always quiet. You could never really tell what he was thinking, you never quite knew where you were with him. Now his father was just the opposite, always very direct, very fair. If there was something wrong with your work he wouldn't beat about the bush, he'd come straight out and tell you. But no one ever resented that, he never tried to make you look small. You always felt afterwards that you'd try to do better in future. Mr Gavin, he had a different personality from his father, he was a lot gentler, but he had that same gift for getting on with people.' She drew a little sigh. 'He was his father's favourite, it was easy to see that.'

She shivered suddenly. 'I've kept you long enough,' Lambert said.

'I'm so glad you called and told me about it,' she said as he stood up to go. 'It would have been a dreadful shock to read it in the evening paper.'

Lambert drove next to Jessup's cottage, a quarter of a mile away. Jessup was a widower, living alone. The gardener had not long come in from his Monday job and was at work in his own back garden when Lambert called. He came into the house and stood washing his hands at the sink in his neatly regimented kitchen while Lambert said his piece. He had heard nothing of what had happened at Eastwood. He stopped washing his hands and turned to look at Lambert with a face of incredulity.

'Good God!' he said. 'You're not telling me Mr Elliott's been murdered?'

When he did at last take it in he sat heavily down on a stool. He pulled a towel from a hook and began to dry his hands in an abstracted fashion. 'Do you think you could find me a drop of brandy?' he said. 'It's in the sideboard in the other room.'

Lambert found the bottle and poured him a measure. Jessup took several rapid swallows. 'It's been a nasty shock,' he said as he set down his glass.

No, he never went to Eastwood on a Friday, or at weekends. Tuesdays, Wednesdays and Thursdays, those were his Eastwood days, summer and winter. 'Thursday evenings I always stayed on till Mr Elliott got home. For my wages, and to talk things over. Mr Elliott used to walk round the garden with me, see what I'd done, tell me what he wanted doing next.' He stared down at the floor. 'He was a very decent young chap. It's hard to think he's gone.'

He looked up at Lambert. 'It's only a month or two back when he said to me, one Thursday evening, that was, he said: "I brought a young lady over on Saturday morning to show her the garden." He said she liked it very much, she particularly liked the heather garden with all the different colours. Mr Elliott seemed very pleased, very happy, the way he said it I began to think maybe we'd be hearing more about the young lady, maybe he was thinking of getting married.'

No, he had never heard mention of any intruder, never seen anyone hanging round the property. He wasn't aware of any disagreement between Elliott and Mr Picton. He had never had anything to do with Picton himself, there had never been any occasion. 'Mrs Cutler used to turf Emily out of the garden if she caught her sneaking round,' he said. 'Emily nips over the wall, plenty of trees and shrubs for her to get over.' He pulled down the corners of his mouth. 'No flies on that young lady. Sharp as a needle.'

He had waited for his money as usual last Thursday evening but Mr Elliott hadn't walked round the garden with him. 'He was full up of a cold, not at all well. I told him he should get to bed and he said: "I intend to. I'm going to dose myself with whisky and lemon and sleep it off." '

Jessup looked closely at the raincoat. 'I can't be sure,' he said at last. 'Mr Elliott sometimes used to slip a raincoat on when he walked round the garden with me.' No, he was sorry but he couldn't be certain one way or the other.

As Lambert was leaving, Jessup said, 'Do you know what'll happen now up at Eastwood? Will they be selling the place?'

'I'm afraid I can't tell you anything about that,' Lambert said.

'I was wondering if I should keep on going up there, to keep the garden tidy. They wouldn't want it turning into a jungle, not if they want to sell it. It doesn't take long for it to get out of hand.'

'I dare say someone'll be in touch with you,' Lambert said. 'Mr Howard Elliott, perhaps, Mr Gavin's brother. Do you know him?'

Jessup shook his head. 'Never met the gentleman. I didn't even know Mr Elliott had a brother.'

The post mortem ended shortly before five. The pathologist was a grey-haired man coming to the end of his career. 'This modern style of burglar,' he said with a long sigh and a shake of his head as he walked along the corridor with Chief-Inspector Kelsey. The Chief gave an indeterminate grunt; whatever the superficial aspects of the case, he was very far from ready at this stage to set it down as a murder committed in the course of burglary. 'At one time,' the pathologist said, 'a burglar only ever struck if he was cornered or attacked. Now . . .' He sighed again. 'It seems to be violence for the sake of violence, utterly pointless. Scarcely a week goes by but we have a case of this sort. I won't be sorry when I retire next year,' he said. 'I find it all more and more deeply depressing, totally inexplicable.'

They reached the door. 'The blow that killed Elliott,' Kelsey said. 'It surely argues someone who knew what he was doing.'

The pathologist opened the door and stood looking out at the pallid sunlight. 'Or someone who was prepared to go to some trouble beforehand to find out.'

The Caprice restaurant was situated half a mile out of Cannonbridge, in a large Regency house that had been a private dwelling until twenty years ago; it was patronized by the well-to-do and discriminating from within a radius of fifty miles or more.

But there were no patrons in evidence when Lambert walked in through the doors; the restaurant closed after lunch and wouldn't open again for another couple of hours. At the reception desk he asked if he could speak to the head waiter. 'He's off duty till six,' the woman told him. Lambert inquired where he might be found. 'He has a flat about a quarter of a mile along the road,' she said. 'Back towards Cannonbridge.' She gave him the address.

The flat turned out to be the converted basement of a Victorian house on the main road. The head waiter was sitting in front of his television set when Lambert rang his bell; he had been watching racing and had fallen into a doze. He came shuffling to the door in carpet slippers, yawning, rubbing his eyes.

Lambert declared his identity and the waiter looked at him with the resigned air of a man who has more than once in the course of his work been asked questions by policemen, inquiry agents of one kind or another. 'You'd better come inside,' he said without enthusiasm.

Lambert followed him into the sitting-room and produced his photographs of Sandra Knightly. 'Ever seen her before?' he asked.

The waiter gave a vast noisy yawn that he didn't bother to conceal. 'Yes, several times.' He wasn't in the least interested in the face before him or in why the police might be asking questions. All he wanted was to be done with Lambert, not waste any more of his brief stretch of leisure. 'She used to come into the Caprice quite a bit at one time, two or three times a week.'

'When would that be?'

'A year, fifteen months ago.'

'Did she come alone?'

'No, she always came with Mr Elliott—from Eastwood. I never saw her with anyone else.' He gave another fleeting look at the photos before putting them down on the table. 'Pretty enough, nothing special.'

'Over what period of time did she come to the restaurant with Elliott?'

'Three or four months, then all of a sudden they stopped. He kept coming of course, he uses the Caprice quite a bit, business dinners, a few friends, that sort of thing. And he often comes on his own.'

'Did he start bringing another young woman?'

'Not for some time, then it was different ones, no special one. It'd be someone new for two or three weeks, then you wouldn't see her again. Sometimes there'd be a stretch when he didn't bring any young woman at all— but he still kept coming with his business friends, of course. Just lately it's been the Neale girl.'

'The Neale girl?'

'Young Miss Neale, from Berrowhill. Her family often come here, they do a lot of entertaining.'

Lambert picked up the photographs. 'Thanks for your help,' he said. 'Don't bother to come to the door, I can see myself out.' But the waiter had already switched on the television again and was on his way to the kitchen to make himself a cup of tea.

There were ten minutes to spare when Lambert reached the main Cannonbridge police station. Kelsey was in his office, brooding over the files; he glanced up at Lambert with an abstracted look. Lambert set down the photographs in front of him and began an account of his afternoon.

'There was a lot more between Sandra Knightly and Gavin Elliott than she would have us believe,' he said. Kelsey studied the photographs as he listened. Sandra in a tailored suit, sitting at the wheel of a car, delivering Christmas presents to old folk; Sandra in a check shirt and jeans, standing in the doorway of an empty shop, organizing a petition against the demolition of a crumbling early Victorian terrace of workmen's dwellings in a nearby street.

Kelsey suddenly threw the photos down on the desk. 'You can forget Knightly,' he said. He jabbed a finger at the second photograph. Sandra smiling full face at the camera, and in the background, framed in the window of the shop, Frank Knightly sitting at a table with a petition sheet laid out before him, heading the list with his own signature.

'Left-handed,' Kelsey said. 'Whoever killed Elliott was right-handed. Not a shadow of doubt.'

The last of the sunlight had vanished as Sergeant Lambert turned the car in through the handsome wrought-iron gates of Claremont. Beside him in the passenger seat the Chief stared out at the garden. It had a well-kept, long-established look.

Lambert slid the car to a halt by the front door. Kelsey got out and stood looking up at the house; beautifully proportioned, well maintained. Lambert pressed the bell and they were admitted by Howard Elliott.

Howard took the two men into a sitting-room. 'I'll tell my wife you're here,' he said. 'She's upstairs, resting. It's been a great shock to her.'

When he had gone Kelsey glanced round the room. Some large oil paintings, mostly landscapes, in ornate gilt frames. To the right of the hearth a portrait of a seated woman, her hands clasped in her lap. Unmistakably an Englishwoman, twenty-three or four years old, a dress and hairstyle suggestive of the years just before the Second World War. Handsome enough in a cool, well-bred fashion; a somewhat critical, aloof air. Not a lady to cuddle up to on a cold winter's night, in the Chief's opinion. 'Mrs Matthew Elliott,' he said to Lambert. 'Howard's mother.' He remembered her twenty or thirty years after the period of the portrait. Her figure had thickened by then, her skin grown faintly lined, the set of her features more rigid, her colouring a little faded.

On top of a display cabinet was a long silver frame with three inset photographs: a wedding photograph of Howard's parents, Matthew very handsome, his bride composed and elegant; Mrs Elliott with a baby in her arms, presumably Howard, both of them smiling; Howard as a boy of eight or nine, standing stiffly beside his mother who sat facing the camera in a formal pose. Kelsey looked round the room; there was no portrait of any other woman, no photograph or drawing of Howard's wife.

There was the sound of footsteps on the stairs, the murmur of voices. A few moments later Howard came into the room with his wife. As he got to his feet Lambert glanced at her and then at the portrait by the fireplace. Judith Elliott could have been an older sister of Howard's mother as a young woman.

Howard introduced his wife and Judith took her seat in an easy chair. She had clearly been crying but apart from a pinkness in her cheeks and some puffiness round her eyes, her appearance was trim and neat. 'I won't keep you any longer than is necessary,' Kelsey said. She nodded without speaking.

Howard offered them drinks which the Chief refused. Judith asked for whisky and water; her voice was deep-toned, surprisingly steady. Howard set the glass down on a small table beside her. She picked it up and took a drink. She didn't ask any questions or volunteer any observations.

Kelsey told them the results of the post mortem briefly and simply; he had no wish to inspire a fainting-fit on the part of Mrs Elliott. Judith showed no reaction, she continued to sip her drink. 'It isn't possible to be exact about the time of death,' Kelsey said. Gavin had drunk a considerable quantity of alcohol and that, apart from lemon juice, black coffee and aspirin, appeared to be all that had passed his lips during his last twenty-four hours. 'The closest we can come to it is that he probably died at some time between five o'clock on Friday afternoon and three o'clock on Saturday morning.'

Howard shot him a surprised glance. But surely, the glance said, I told you I spoke to Gavin around seven or eight on Friday evening; that must surely set the earlier limit at seven, not five.

'I'm giving you the results of the post mortem,' Kelsey said in answer to that glance, 'not the results of the police investigation.' Howard moved his head in response but looked less than satisfied. At the end of the post mortem Kelsey had in fact pressed the pathologist on that point but the pathologist had refused to budge from his assessment. 'Could you perhaps lean more towards the earlier part of the period?' Kelsey had persisted. 'Say, around ten or eleven?' But the pathologist had remained obdurate. 'I can't be in any way more precise,' he said. 'I couldn't stand by it in court.'

Kelsey asked Judith if she could recognize the raincoat. She gave it a couple of swift glances and shook her head.

'You've scarcely looked at it,' Kelsey said gently.

'I've never seen it before,' she said on a note of obstinacy.

He felt it wise to give a preliminary warning before producing the knife in its plastic envelope. Judith took a long drink before she slid a glance at the narrow blade, the rosewood handle. The knife was Sheffield made, not new but little used; it was razor-sharp.

Judith gave a quick shake of her head. She drained her glass and held it out in silence to her husband; he rose and refilled it.

Kelsey didn't press her about the knife. He asked Howard if he had seen it before. Howard considered the knife with an air of calm detachment. 'I can't say that I have,' he said judicially, 'but there's nothing very distinctive about it. I imagine you could buy one like it in any department store. I believe we have some knives here that are very similar.' He could have been discussing some commonplace item of household cutlery. Nor had he displayed any emotion earlier when he identified Gavin's body.

Kelsey asked Judith if she knew of any particular female friend of Gavin's.

'There's a girl over at Berrowhill,' she said. 'Charlotte Neale. Gavin liked her a lot.' She looked at the Chief, her large blue-grey eyes full of pain. 'I think she's the type he might have thought of marrying.'

'This visit to your godmother,' Kelsey said. 'When was it arranged?'

'About ten days ago. It was her seventieth birthday.'

'When did you go over there?'

'On Thursday. I got there just before lunch. Howard came over on Saturday morning.'

'And you went over to see your brother on Friday evening,' Kelsey said to Howard in the same easy tone.

Howard was looking at his wife. His head jerked

round. 'No,' he said in a tone of some surprise. 'I didn't go to see Gavin, I phoned him around seven or eight, I offered to go over but he said it wasn't necessary.' He frowned. 'Surely I told you all this this morning, at the office?'

'Oh yes,' Kelsey said. 'I believe you did.'

When they left Howard walked with them to the door, and stood watching as Lambert set the car in motion.

'The blow that killed Elliott,' Lambert said as he drove out through the gates. 'Did the pathologist think it was struck by a man?'

'Man or woman,' Kelsey said. 'It could have been either.'

They reached the main road and Lambert had to concentrate on the traffic. A minute or two later he said, 'Would you call Judith Elliott attractive?' He wasn't greatly taken by the lady himself but experience had taught him that the Chief, basing his standards on principles utterly mystifying to Lambert, might have different ideas.

Kelsey gazed out at the hedges flying past. 'Yes,' he said after a moment. 'I should think she's capable of being very attractive—to the right man. When she chooses.'

CHAPTER 8

When Kelsey arrived at the Cannonbridge branch of Elliott Gilmore at eight-thirty on Tuesday morning Miss Tapsell had already been in the building for a quarter of an hour. During that time she had passed on to Mrs Worrall, the cleaner, such scanty details of Gavin's death as she possessed, together with the Chief's request that Mrs Worrall should stay until he arrived. She also—much to the Chief's annoyance when he perceived what had happened—gave Mrs Worrall the benefit of her opinions about the dark grey raincoat and its origins, giving these opinions, moreover, in a fashion that instantly aroused in Mrs Worrall a powerful desire to express a totally opposite point of view.

The Chief spent barely two minutes talking to the cleaner before he realized he was wasting his time. Once Mrs Worrall understood that Miss Tapsell had firmly stated her belief—hardened overnight into unshakable certainty—that the raincoat had belonged to Mr Elliott and had hung in the basement cupboard, nothing would induce her to say that she had ever seen the garment or knew anything about it; she certainly had never seen it hanging up in her cubbyhole.

'This is very important,' Kelsey said in a last despairing throw. 'This piece of evidence could be the key to the whole case. I want you to think again and think very carefully.' But Mrs Worrall was already setting her lips and shaking her head. 'Miss Tapsell is equally certain that she did see it in the cupboard,' Kelsey persisted.

Mrs Worrall jerked her shoulders. 'It wouldn't be the first time I've known Miss Tapsell to say for certain something that turned out afterwards to be a load of claptrap,' she said with mulish stubbornness. And Kelsey was forced to leave it at that.

'Infuriating pair of women,' he said sourly as Lambert drove him over to Martleigh later in the morning. 'It's my belief Mrs Worrall did see the raincoat but no power on earth's going to make her say so now.' He blew out a long breath of exasperation.

His temper was in no way sweetened by the hold-ups on the carriageway. By the time they had covered the twenty-two miles he had to take a grip on himself to force a reasonably amiable expression on to his countenance as they walked up the steps of Elliott Gilmore.

Roche was expecting them. He came into the reception

hall and shook hands. Kelsey gave him a swift assessing look. Medium height, wiry build, a sharp-looking customer.

'This is a dreadful business,' Roche said as he took them into his office. He put himself and his staff at the Chief's disposal.

The atmosphere in the offices was subdued and serious but didn't manifest the same air of shock that Kelsey had felt yesterday in the other two branches. The lapse of twenty-four hours, no doubt, together with the fact that the staff here—a third the size of that at the main branch—had been recruited locally a bare twelve months ago and had scarcely any contact with Gavin Elliott.

Kelsey wasn't surprised that his talk to the staff elicited nothing of any value; one clerk had never even laid eyes on the dead man. Certainly no one was able to recognize the raincoat or the knife; nor could Roche offer any assistance on these points.

'This Chamber of Commerce dinner you attended instead of Elliott,' Kelsey said. 'What time did you get there?'

'It was at the Northgrove Hotel,' Roche said. 'I got there about a quarter to eight, the dinner started at eight.'

'And what time did you leave the hotel?'

'Shortly before midnight. There were still a few folk there, drinking and talking.'

'Had you any reason for leaving early?'

Roche smiled slightly. 'I don't know that I'd call it early. Four hours of that sort of evening always strikes me as plenty. I never stay to the end. And I had to get up for work the next morning, I was doing the Saturday stint here.'

'If you could give me the names of two or three of the other guests,' Kelsey said. 'Routine, you understand.'

'Yes, of course.' Roche supplied the details. He could tell the Chief little about Gavin's personal life. 'I didn't see much of him outside business,' he said.

When Kelsey asked if he knew of any disagreements with clients, Roche said after a moment, 'There was some argument with a neighbour, a chap called Picton. But he wasn't a client of the firm and Gavin was determined he shouldn't try to make out he was.' He outlined what Gavin had told him about Picton; it squared with what Kelsey had already been told.

'Do you think Gavin was worried about it?'

'He certainly mentioned it a little more seriously the last time I was over in Cannonbridge for a Friday meeting—that was ten days ago. But even then he was half joking about it.'

Kelsey had appointments in Cannonbridge for the afternoon with Elliott's bank and solicitor. 'You'd better trot along to Roche's digs after you leave here,' he told Lambert. 'Have a word with his landlady, check his times and so on, for last Friday evening.'

As Lambert walked to his car shortly after two he looked at the name and address Miss Tapsell had given them: Mrs Nugent, 72 Greatfield Road. He stopped at a newsagent's and learned that the road was close at hand. 'Won't take you five minutes in the car,' the newsagent said. 'You could walk it in ten.'

Greatfield Road was in a quiet residential area. No. 72 stood on a corner; a detached Victorian house in good trim, with a small front garden. It all looked presentable enough.

He had to press the bell two or three times before the door was at last opened by a woman in her sixties. Her face was a little flushed. She put up a hand and patted her hair, tightly curled, tinted a deep coffee brown, with a line of white showing along the roots. She looked out at Lambert without speaking.

'Mrs Nugent?' he said and she nodded. He introduced

himself. 'I believe you have a Mr Stephen Roche lodging with you?' Her face creased into lines of anxiety. 'It's all right,' he added. 'It's nothing to worry about. Nothing's happened to Mr Roche, he isn't in any kind of trouble. Just a routine check in connection with a case I'm working on, one or two details you might be able to help us with.'

Her face relaxed. She put a hand on her heart. 'I get upset so easily these days,' she said with apology. 'I've been the same ever since my husband died eighteen months ago. He had a heart attack and went all in a minute. It was so sudden, such a terrible shock.' She drew a long quivering breath. 'I was upstairs trying to get a little nap when you rang.'

'I'm sorry I disturbed you,' Lambert said gently. 'Do you think I could step inside for a moment? I won't keep you long.'

'Yes, do come in.' She led the way along the hall. 'That's Mr Roche's sitting-room. He does a lot of writing and paperwork in the evenings, studying and reading.' She gestured at a door on the left. 'I keep this one for myself.' She ushered him into a pleasant, sunny room, comfortably furnished, scrupulously clean, a bowl of daffodils in flower by the window. 'I'm not much of a reader myself,' she said. 'I like to watch television in the evenings, it helps to take your mind off things.'

He sat down opposite her. 'If I could just confirm a couple of dates and times, then I'll get off, out of your way. Last Friday night — was Mr Roche here?'

'Yes, he was. He should have been going home but he had to go to a dinner unexpectedly so he stayed over till the Saturday.' He had come in from the office as usual, just after six, he had bathed and changed, left the house at about seven-fifteen; he had returned around a quarter past twelve. She had seen and spoken to him after he returned, he had gone straight to bed. In the morning he left the house at eight-fifteen, taking his suitcase with him to the office. He came back from Cannonbridge as usual on Sunday evening, shortly before ten o'clock.

'That's all I want to know,' Lambert said. 'Thank you for your help.'

She looked faintly uneasy. 'Does Mr Roche know you're here asking questions about him?' she said as Lambert got to his feet.

'Oh, that's all right,' he said cheerfully. 'You've no need to make a secret of it. This is just normal routine, Mr Roche won't mind in the least. We have to do this kind of thing every day, check everything a dozen times over.'

Kelsey's appointment with Gavin Elliott's solicitors was not till a quarter to four so he called first at the bank in Market Street, the bank old Matthew Elliott had always used and which still handled the firm's account.

'An appalling business,' the manager said. 'A young man like that, his whole life before him.'

There was certainly nothing amiss with the financial side of Elliott Gilmore, he assured the Chief. No juggling between one account and another, no overstretching, overborrowing, no tricky deals, everything as sound as a bell. 'Gavin was trained by his father,' he said, 'and Matthew Elliott was a first-class businessman.'

Kelsey scrutinized the records of Gavin's personal account. 'You can read a man's private life from his bank statements,' a manager had said to Kelsey once, years ago, and the Chief had ever afterwards tried to interpret statements in that light—not always with much success. They usually seemed a commonplace list of payments for mortgages, rates, fuel, insurance, groceries, holidays and all the other essentials of daily life.

Gavin Elliott's statements contained no mysterious debits or credits, nothing to set the imagination working, just straightforward payments to department stores, travel agents, outfitters, restaurants, clubs, jewellers, wine merchants. And a dozen other mundane outgoings.

Elliott's solicitors were Munslow and Newbould, a long-established firm that had been his father's solicitors and still acted for the firm. Kelsey was shown into an office where Mr Munslow, a shrewd-eyed, urbane-looking man of around fifty, was expecting him.

'It's only a couple of weeks since I was chatting to Gavin,' Munslow told the Chief. 'He was full of plans for the business.'

No, Gavin had carried no life insurance. But he had made a will.

'When was it made?' Kelsey asked.

Munslow opened a box file, took out a document, unfolded and examined it. 'In January of last year. I strongly advised him to make a will earlier, when he inherited his father's estate three years ago, but he put it off.' He shook his head. 'Young men, they never see any need for haste in these matters.'

'Any particular reason why he decided to make a will at that time?'

'It was after Howard came back into the firm. He'd been back three or four months and Gavin felt he'd settled down, everything was going well. He believed the arrangement was a success, that it would last. He told me he hoped to get married one day and then of course he'd make a new will; he hoped he'd have a son to inherit the business.' He looked down at the document. 'He intended this to be an interim will. It's very straightforward. Apart from a few minor bequests, the whole of his estate, the business, the house, his investments, personal possessions, everything, lock, stock and barrel, goes to his half-brother, Howard Elliott.'

CHAPTER 9

The inquest on Gavin Elliott was set down for Wednesday afternoon. Chief-Inspector Kelsey sat in his office on Wednesday morning casting a brooding eye forward to three o'clock. The proceedings would be brief and formal, without a doubt, the inquest opened and adjourned.

'You can get over to the Wychford office,' he said to Lambert. 'Finish up over there.' Apart from the men going through the books and files—nothing to do with Lambert. 'I'll get along to the main office again,' Kelsey added. He intended spending no further time at the Martleigh branch, unless something fresh turned up. Which reminded him. 'Better check those names Stephen Roche gave us,' he said. 'The men who were with him at the dinner. Get that out of the way, then get over to Wychford.'

By ten o'clock Lambert was on his way. He had checked with the men Roche had named and everything squared. He contemplated the rest of the morning, suddenly remembering Mrs Dolphin with her made-up eyes and youthful clothes. I'll take her to lunch, he decided, shouldn't be much difficulty fixing it up. She didn't strike him as the type to go off to lunch every day with a bosom pal. She seemed far more likely to have quarrelled at some time or other with everyone on the staff, to exist there on terms of armed neutrality.

He had observed on his previous visit that the staff lunch-times were staggered, to avoid closing the office; Mrs Dolphin had gone off, alone, at one-fifteen.

The morning went swiftly by. Howard Elliott was out most of the time and the rest of the staff seemed to be resuming a good part of their usual work routines, in spite of the disruptions. By one o'clock Lambert had more or less finished. Five minutes later he paused by Mrs Dolphin's desk.

'I'm off in a few minutes,' he told her in a low, matey tone. 'I wondered if you knew anywhere decent for lunch? Not too expensive, on my pay, a good pub, maybe.' He gave her the eye. 'You look like a lady who'd know a good place.' I bet there isn't a pub in Wychford she doesn't know inside out, he thought.

She gave him back a swift assessing look; he saw she'd swallowed the bait. 'There's the Feathers,' she said in an equally low conspiratorial tone. 'The food's quite good, there's always a couple of hot dishes.'

'Sounds just the ticket. I don't know if you'd care to join me?' He gave her a smile, the up-and-coming young man with an eye for an attractive woman of the world. 'I hate eating alone if there's a chance of eating with a good-looking woman.'

She moved her head and smiled. 'All right.' She looked at her watch. 'I'm off in five minutes.'

'Right. I'll meet you there.'

She glanced about the room at the other clerks. 'Twenty past one,' she said in a discreet undertone. 'In the lounge bar.' She bent her head again over her papers.

At one-fifteen Lambert entered the lounge bar of the Feathers and sat down. The last time he'd been here was six months ago. He'd been accompanied then by a dashing young woman — departed now, alas! to other scenes and other embraces. He gave a little sigh, lost for a moment in a recollection of laughter on autumn evenings, her soft hair and warm skin. He suddenly became aware of someone standing beside him, speaking to him. He glanced up and saw Mrs Dolphin looking down at him with a bright smile.

'You were miles away,' she said on a flirtatious, rallying note.

He sprang to his feet. 'I'm sorry. What can I get you?' He thrust the dashing young lady to the back of his mind where she continued to lurk during the next forty minutes, popping suddenly out from time to time when a drift of perfume or the sound of a voice touched a chord of memory. By dint of concentrating on the food—quite eatable—and the enduring charms of Mrs Dolphin's legs, he managed to give sufficient attention to whatever she might be disposed to tell him.

But first there was information she clearly intended to elicit from him. By the time they were half way through their chilli con carne she had learned that he wasn't a native of Cannonbridge but came from the other side of the county, that he wasn't married, he lived in digs, and had at present no serious girlfriend; she also knew how he liked to spend such free time as he managed to snatch. She plainly intended to suggest that some of this free time might profitably be spent with her. Not if I can help it, Lambert thought, smiling resolutely back at her with a roguish eye.

She'd been married once, a long time ago, had divorced her husband after a couple of years. 'Gambling,' she said. 'Absolutely hopeless. He'd have gambled the clothes off my back.' She stared moodily down at her plate.

'Have another drink,' Lambert said.

He came back with it and set it down on the table. Her face still wore a brooding look. Time to change the conversation. As he took his seat again he asked her casually how long she had worked at Elliott Gilmore.

'I've always worked there,' she told him. 'Ever since I left school.'

'Did you know the old man? Matthew Elliott?'

'I didn't actually know him, I never worked for him, but he used to come over to Wychford sometimes, to the office.' She pulled a face. 'But we all knew what he was like.' She flicked a glance at Lambert. 'You know about the divorce and all that?'

'I know something,' he said. 'Not a great deal.'

She leaned forward with a glint in her eye. 'He'd been keeping this other woman for years, he'd managed to keep it all nice and quiet. Then one day the balloon went up. He and his lady love were in bed one night and the cottage down the lane went on fire. He was no end of a hero. He rushed into the cottage and dragged out the old lady who lived there. He got himself a few burns in the process, had to have hospital treatment. Of course the papers got hold of it. He knew the jig was up so he made a clean breast of the whole thing to his wife.' She gave Lambert a look of massive cynicism. 'You can't tell me his wife didn't know all along that he was having a bit on the side. I reckon it suited her to keep her eyes shut. She didn't mind what he got up to as long as she could pretend she didn't know about it. But when it did come out into the open—' She laughed. 'Talk about an uproar!'

'Were you surprised when Howard came back into the firm?'

'I was absolutely staggered! It was the last thing in the world I'd ever have expected him to do, come back and play second fiddle to a younger brother born on the wrong side of the blanket.'

'Do you know his wife?'

'Not personally.' She pulled a face. 'I don't move in those circles. I've seen her about, of course, always dolled up to the nines.' She took out a handkerchief and dabbed her lips. 'She was no one, the daughter of some retired Army major without two pennies to rub together.' She gave a little sideways jerk of her head. 'She's got plenty now she's Mrs Howard Elliott. I hope she's pleased with her bargain.' She opened her handbag and searched for a lipstick. 'Real mother's boy, Howard. Wouldn't suit me.'

She grinned. 'Except for the money, I wouldn't say no to that.'

The wall clock struck two as she finished repairing her make-up. 'I'll have to be getting back,' she said. 'I'll give you my address. And my phone number. I've got a nice little flat half a mile from here.' She tore a page from a diary and scribbled down the address. 'Give me a ring. Any evening.'

He left the pub with her and stood watching as she walked up the road, admiring the rear view of her long elegant legs. After a few yards she looked back and gave him a wave. He raised his hand in reply.

As he made his way across to the car park he screwed up the piece of paper without looking at it and dropped it into a litter bin.

There were no surprises at the inquest. Lambert stood waiting for the Chief at the foot of the steps leading down from the Cannonbridge court house. The Chief was standing in the doorway, talking to an official. Howard Elliott glanced at Kelsey as he went past him and received a nod and a lift of the hand in reply; Judith Elliott hadn't attended the proceedings. Leonard Picton was there, and Mrs Cutler, together with a number of sightseers and curiosity-mongers, several faces Kelsey remembered from Littlebourne village — and members of the press.

He shook his head as he came down the steps; nothing to say yet, far too soon. He continued to shake his head as he joined Lambert and they made their way to where the car was parked. A cold wind had sprung up, it blew in their faces as they crossed the open ground.

'Did you notice Picton in court?' Kelsey asked Lambert when they had shaken off the reporters. 'He was taking a very keen interest in the proceedings.' They reached the car. 'Time we paid a little more attention to that gentleman,' he said as he got in and settled himself back. 'We'll get over to Ellenborough tomorrow, see what they thought of him there.'

The college at which Leonard Picton had taught before taking up his appointment in Cannonbridge stood on the outskirts of Ellenborough. A large Edwardian building with ample grounds and playing-fields. 'It's twice the size of the Cannonbridge college,' Kelsey said as Lambert halted the car by the front entrance on Thursday morning. They walked up the steps and in through the swing doors; a clock in the entrance hall showed five minutes past ten.

They had no appointment, had made no contact with the college. 'I'm afraid the Principal isn't here today,' his secretary told the Chief. 'He's away at a conference, and the Vice-Principal is at home, in bed with 'flu.' She smiled cheerfully. 'You could speak to the head of Liberal Studies, she's holding the fort.'

She showed them into a waiting-room. She came back a few minutes later and took them along a corridor to an office where a young woman sat behind a desk. She stood up and came round the desk. She was in her early thirties and was dressed like a student, in a sweater and denim skirt.

'Sorry everyone's away,' she said. Kelsey introduced himself and Lambert. 'Coppers,' she said with a little sideways inclination of her head. 'One of the students been running amok?' She perched herself on the desk and crossed her legs, very long, beautiful legs; Lambert could scarcely keep his eyes off them.

'It's nothing to do with any of your students,' Kelsey told her. She was the kind of young woman who always made him feel uneasy, as if he'd committed some sin he'd managed until now to conceal, but couldn't at the moment quite recall. To Sergeant Lambert, on the other hand, she was the kind of young woman who made him feel there might yet be hope for the world.

The Chief explained that he would like some information about a Mr Leonard Picton. 'I understand he was on the staff here until a couple of years ago,' he said.

'Oh yes, Leonard Picton,' she said at once with lively interest. 'We remember Leonard Picton very well, a difficult man to forget. What's he been up to? Clouting one of his students? Or thumping a parent?' Kelsey made no reply. 'Maybe you just don't like the look of him,' she said. 'Neither do I. Or any of the rest of the staff here.'

'Why did he leave?'

'Because he'd have been booted out through the door if he hadn't left.' She laughed. 'You can't ask for a better reason than that.'

'Why should they want to boot him out?'

'Because he was a pain in the neck. I was only here a year or so before he left, but it was long enough. I gather there were several episodes of one kind and another before I came here: trouble with members of staff, parents, students, even the caretaker.'

'Why didn't they get rid of him earlier?'

She pulled a face. 'It's not all that easy in this profession. Simple enough if you steal the petty cash or seduce a student, but Picton wasn't given to either of those peccadilloes.'

'How did they manage it in the end?'

'He had one of his arguments with a student in class over some point in his lecture, and Picton flung a book at the student. Flung it with some force. The student ducked and the book shattered a window. You never heard such rejoicing in the staff room. At last he'd committed a fatal error, he'd damaged Government property. He was told he could either find himself another job pronto, or he'd be sacked—and up in court, into the bargain. So he found himself another job—in Cannonbridge.'

'Hardly seems fair to Cannonbridge,' Kelsey observed.

She moved her shoulders. 'He came here with a good reference from his last college, never a word about temperamental difficulties. He has a good degree, he knows his stuff, he's a pretty fair historian. We sent him on his way with an equally good reference.' She grinned. 'That's the way the game is played. How else would anyone ever get rid of someone like that?'

She jumped down from the desk, her long black hair swinging against her slender neck. 'The abiding memory he left behind him here,' she said, 'is of a clever bastard. A devious and cunning sod.'

It was almost four when Sergeant Lambert pulled up outside the gate of Manor Cottage. He glanced over in the direction of Eastwood. 'I was thinking,' he said. 'If it was a burglar, do you think Mrs Cutler might have put him on to it—intentionally or unintentionally?'

Kelsey looked at him in silence.

'She may go out for a drink in the evening,' Lambert said. 'She may play bingo, chatter with her neighbours.' Easy enough in all innocence to let fall a word or two about Eastwood, the treasures she dusted daily.

'It's certainly possible,' Kelsey said. 'We'll pop along and have a word with her after we've finished here.' He glanced at his watch. 'Yes,' he said on a more decisive note. 'We'll do that. See how she lives, how she spends her evenings. There might be something in it.' They got out of the car and walked up the front path.

Olive Picton was in the kitchen, as usual at this time of day, engaged in long and laborious preparation of the evening meal. Leonard was upstairs in his study, finishing his notes for his next class, and so exempt from all such mundane interruptions as answering the front door. Emily had not yet come in from school.

When Olive heard their knock she cast a rapid eye over the pans on the cooker. She snatched up a towel and dried her hands, red and rough from the cold water in which she had been scrubbing vegetables, and went swiftly along the passage to the front door.

'We'd like another word with you and your husband,' Kelsey told her. 'If it isn't inconvenient.' She made a gesture of acquiescence and held the door wide for them to enter. At the sound of their voices Picton's head appeared round the study door. 'If you could spare us a few minutes,' the Chief called up to him.

'Yes, of course,' Picton answered readily.

'Would you mind if we talked in the kitchen?' Mrs Picton asked as her husband came down the stairs. 'I'm in the middle of cooking.' A smell of baking drifted into the passage and Lambert turned at once, like a pointer, when the seductive fragrance reached his nostrils.

'Just a few details to clear up,' Kelsey said amiably as they all followed Mrs Picton into the kitchen. 'They crop up all the time in these cases.'

Picton pulled forward a couple of chairs. 'I have a class at the college at five,' he said. He didn't sit down himself but stood with his back to the window, his hands clasped behind him, his expression controlled and wary under a surface pleasantness.

Kelsey sat down. 'That's all right,' he said. 'We won't keep you long.'

On the stove a pan of grain began to heave and sigh, ejecting fierce little spurts towards the ceiling. Mrs Picton went hurriedly over and stirred the energy out of it.

'To get back to last Friday night,' Kelsey said. 'You've both had time to talk things over, cast your minds back. You may have remembered some detail. Can either of you recall hearing a vehicle arrive next door on Friday evening, or at any time during Friday night?' Mrs Picton shook her head and continued her stirring.

'A certain amount of traffic goes by here,' Picton said. 'I doubt if we'd notice.'

'Can you remember seeing any lights on at Eastwood that evening, or during the night?' Again Mrs Picton shook her head. Picton made a little irritated movement of his hand but answered in a voice he strove to keep light and good-tempered. 'Again, we wouldn't expect to notice. I doubt if either of us glanced that way. We're not the type to go spying on neighbours, we've better things to do.'

Kelsey gave him a long look. 'But you did see fit to hang about the Eastwood garden to voice your grievances.'

'That's a gross exaggeration,' Picton said at once with lively protest. 'And in any case it was an entirely different matter. That was to do with a specific point of business, nothing to do with Elliott's private life, with noticing cars arriving or whether lights were on or off.'

'What did you mean by saying two could play at that game?' Kelsey said suddenly.

Picton's head jerked back. He stood biting his top lip, looking at the Chief without speaking.

' "Cut me dead, would you?" ' the Chief said. ' "Two can play at that game! Watch out I don't cut you down to size!" That was what you said to Elliott one day last week, when he got out of his car to open the gate. What did you mean by it?'

Picton managed a smile of sorts. His teeth were uneven, very white. 'It was just a manner of speaking. The heat of the moment. It didn't mean anything.'

'Precisely what was in your mind when you said those words?' Kelsey persisted.

Picton moved his shoulders. 'I suppose I had been influenced to some extent by Elliott's opinions when I made some investments. I suppose it did just cross my mind that if they didn't pick up there could be some possibility that I might be able to sue him. Just a passing thought, more a technical point than anything.'

'Is it your intention now to sue the firm?' Kelsey asked.

'Or Elliott's estate?'

Picton shook his head with energy. 'Good Lord, no. When I thought about it later, I realized I wouldn't have any sort of a case.' He smiled. 'And anyway, I'm confident the market will recover. I won't be out of pocket in the end.'

Mrs Picton crossed to the side table and picked up a bowl. She tipped the contents into a pan and set it on the stove.

'To get back again to last Friday,' Kelsey said. 'Did either of you wake during the night?' Lambert saw Mrs Picton's hands pause for an instant. She slid a glance at her husband. Picton registered her look.

'Yes, I believe I did wake,' he said after a moment. He fingered his straggling side whiskers. 'Yes, I definitely remember. I got out of bed and went along to the study.'

'Oh?' Kelsey said with sharp interest. 'Had something disturbed you? Some sound from outside?'

'Not that I'm aware of. I often wake in the night. I have an active brain, it doesn't always switch off when I get into bed. If I wake up and find my brain mulling over something, I know I won't get to sleep again for an hour or two, so I usually put on a dressing-gown and go along to the study, do a bit of work till I feel sleepy again.'

'He's done that for years,' Mrs Picton said, her hands busy again at the stove. 'I'm used to it. Mostly I don't hear him, but if I do I just turn over and go straight back to sleep.'

'Did you go outside at all?' Kelsey asked Picton. 'Or glance out?'

Picton shook his head. 'I came down here and made myself a hot drink, then I went up to the study. I didn't notice any noise or disturbance. I didn't go out or look out.'

'What time was all this?'

'I'm afraid I can't be very exact, I don't usually bother

looking at the clock. At a guess I'd say it might be about two or three.'

The pan on the stove came to the boil, giving out a delicate scented aroma that Lambert couldn't place. 'Chestnuts,' Mrs Picton told him in a low conspiratorial tone, seeing his look. 'Dried chestnuts, you have to soak them first.' She drew the pan a little way off the heat.

'How did you spend Friday evening?' Kelsey said. 'The three of you?'

'We were here in the cottage,' Picton answered. 'We spent it much as usual. I did some work in my study, Olive was cooking, sewing, Emily did her homework. Then we read, listened to the radio, watched television, had supper. Emily went to bed as usual at eight-thirty and Olive and I went up about half past ten.'

'And the rest of the weekend?'

'We went to an Ecology conference on Saturday,' Olive said. 'The three of us.' She mentioned a manor house run by a commune that organized such events; it was some fifteen miles away. Kelsey had seen their advertisements in the local paper.

'We left here about eight on Saturday morning,' Picton said. 'We got back around half past eight in the evening.'

'And on Sunday?'

'We went to the wildfowl sanctuary.' This was twenty-odd miles away. 'Emily had been asking to go there. We set off after breakfast.'

'What time did you get back?'

'About seven,' Mrs Picton said. 'We called in to see a working mill on the way back. And cycling home was up-hill most of the way.'

'Cycling?' Kelsey echoed. 'You made both those trips by bicycle?'

She looked surprised. 'Yes, of course. We go every-where by bicycle. Unless the distance is too great; then we use public transport.'

'You have no car?'

'Indeed we do not!' Picton said with force. 'I consider private motoring a criminal waste of resources, it pollutes the atmosphere . . .' He continued in this vein for a minute or two while the smell of baking bread grew stronger and more delicious.

Mrs Picton picked up an oven cloth, opened the oven door and pulled out a loaf tin. She slipped the loaf out on to the table and tapped the underside, which gave back a hollow sound. She gave a little satisfied nod and took the rest of the bread from the oven. Four good-sized loaves, crusty, golden-brown. Lambert couldn't help glancing at them with naked longing.

'Would you like a slice?' she asked him in a low voice as she set the loaves to cool on wire trays. 'With butter and honey?' she added with a fleeting smile. Her teeth were as white as her husband's but a good deal more regular. She didn't look anything like as plain when she smiled.

Lambert was just about to utter a fervent 'Yes, please' when he recollected himself. He glanced at Kelsey and saw that gentleman levelling at him a glare of such ferocity that the words froze on his lips. 'No, thanks,' he managed to say, in a tone of the deepest regret. She gave a little understanding nod.

There was the whirr of a bicycle outside and Emily sailed past the kitchen window. A minute or two later she came in through the back door, her cheeks glowing. 'I knew you were here,' she told Kelsey. 'I saw your car.' Her sharp, bright eyes darted from one to the other of the two policemen. 'You've got a radio in your car,' she said to Lambert. 'May I listen to it?'

'That's enough of that,' her father said firmly. Emily grinned at Lambert. Her teeth had the same glittering, snow-white look as her parents'. All that coarse flour, Lambert thought, probably has a sand-blasting effect. Emily crossed to the stove and sniffed at the chestnuts.

'Have you done any apricots?' she asked her mother. 'I like them with chestnuts.'

'I've got some nectarines and peaches soaking.' Olive nodded at the row of basins. 'I'll put them on to cook shortly, they'll be ready for supper.' Lambert closed his eyes for a moment.

'Do you do all this cooking every day?' Kelsey couldn't refrain from asking.

Mrs Picton opened her mouth but before she could speak her husband answered for her. 'A Frenchwoman goes to the shops three times a day, just to buy fresh bread.' As if that disposed of the matter and his wife's attitude towards it once and for all. Mrs Picton gave the Chief the faintest flick of a smile.

'If there's nothing else,' Picton said, 'it's time I was getting along to the college.'

'There's nothing else at the moment.' Kelsey waved a hand at the garden. 'We'd like to take another look round outside, if you've no objection.'

'Go right ahead,' Picton said amiably. He left the room and they heard him running up the stairs. He came back a few moments later wearing a jacket and carrying a briefcase. He kissed his wife on the cheek. 'I'll be back about seven-thirty,' he told her.

Emily followed her father outside as he went along to the shed for his bicycle. A few minutes later they both passed the window again, Picton wheeling his bicycle and Emily walking beside him, chatting with animation.

'We'll stroll about outside for a few minutes,' the Chief told Mrs Picton. 'Pay no attention to us.'

The air was fresh and sharp after the warmth of the kitchen. They walked down the garden, past a herb bed, a patch of young nettles, rows of fat leeks, elderly sprout plants, mop-headed and yellowing, spring cabbages incurled like dark green rosebuds. Kelsey walked over to the dividing wall. He stepped up on to the exposed roots of a beech and looked across at the Eastwood garden. If someone drove quietly in and parked under the belt of trees, thickly grown, with a wealth of overhanging branches, the Pictons probably wouldn't hear, especially on a windy night, with their radio or television on.

There was a rustle in the shrubbery. Kelsey turned and saw Emily peering out at him like a dryad from the branches of a prunus, her long tawny hair gleaming against the wine-red leaves and pale pink blossom. She jumped down and came over to them.

'Did you know Mr Elliott had a lady friend?' she said with an air of vast importance. Kelsey looked at her without speaking. 'I don't mean Charlotte Neale,' she added. 'Mr Elliott brought Charlotte here a few times but they never stayed in the house, they were always going out or coming back from somewhere. I know who Charlotte is from her photos in the paper, she does a lot of show-jumping.' She widened her eyes at the Chief. 'Mr Elliott had another lady friend. They never went out together. When she came here they always stopped in the house.'

'Who is it you're talking about?' Kelsey said, mastering dislike. In his opinion a good slap now and then would do Emily no harm at all.

'I don't know who she was,' Emily said with a strong note of regret. 'She always came here in the evenings, when it was dark. She used to drive in with her headlights off, just the sidelights on. She always parked over there under the trees. Then she'd go round to the door on the far side, very quickly and quietly, you could hardly see her. I could see the light shining out when the door opened.'

CHAPTER 10

Emily stood looking up at the Chief with pleased expectation.

'And pray how do you know all this?' he said with an edge of distaste in his voice.

She was in no way abashed. 'They always send me to bed at half past eight but I hardly ever go to sleep then, it's far too early. I read or look out of the window. I turn the light off and pull back the curtains.'

'You said this lady used to come here,' Kelsey said. 'Was it some time ago? Had she stopped coming?'

'I haven't seen her since about last November. Then he started bringing Charlotte Neale here.'

'How long had this other lady been coming here?'

'I should think a few months.'

'Did she come regularly?'

'I saw her two or three times a week.'

'Can you describe her?'

She shook her head. 'I only ever saw her in the dark.'

'Did you mention any of this to your parents?' She shook her head again.

'Last Friday evening,' Kelsey said. 'Did you see any cars or callers at Eastwood? Did you see any lights go on in the house?'

'I didn't look out last Friday,' she said at once. 'I went to sleep straight away. We had to get up early to go to the conference.'

'Did you go into the Eastwood garden at all during that weekend?'

'No, I didn't.'

'Are you sure?' he persisted. 'You needn't worry about telling me if you did, I won't tick you off for trespassing.'

'I wasn't there, I'd tell you if I was.' She looked up at him with wide, innocent-seeming eyes. 'We were out all day, Saturday and Sunday.'

'Do you often go out both days at the weekend like that?'

'No.'

'Have you ever done so before?'

'Not that I can remember. Sometimes we go out for one day, or half a day.'

'When was it decided, that you'd all go on these outings?'

'On Friday evening while we were having supper. Daddy said he felt like a break after the winter, he thought the change would do us all good.'

The back door of Manor Cottage opened and Mrs Picton's voice called, 'Emily!'

'Coming!' Emily called back. She darted off without another word.

The Chief stood looking after her. 'One thing's for sure,' he said. 'Picton's arrangements for the weekend made certain that the only person likely to go snooping round Eastwood wasn't about the place.'

'If it was Picton,' Lambert said, 'then where's the loot? Presumably he took the stuff to recompense himself for his losses.' A rough valuation had now been placed on the missing articles, based on the list Mrs Cutler had dictated and the quality of the remaining pieces; the figure was between six and seven thousand pounds. There was certainly no trace of the articles in Manor Cottage or any of its sheds and outhouses.

'Suppose Picton put them in an outhouse on Friday night,' Lambert said. 'He locks the door, keeps the key in his pocket. Then on Saturday night he gets out of bed again, sneaks outside and removes the stuff from the outhouses, takes it right away from the property, puts it somewhere where it can stay safely hidden till everything's over and forgotten.' Kelsey made no reply. 'He was alone when he went into Eastwood on Monday morning,' Lambert said. 'He went up the stairs and into Elliott's bedroom by himself. That would give him a chance to check that he hadn't left incriminating traces, he could remove or add anything he thought necessary.'

Kelsey passed a hand across his jaw. 'He wouldn't need to wait till Monday morning for that. He had Saturday and Sunday nights to go back into the house, refine the crime, repair any oversights.'

Lambert struck the air with his fist. 'That could explain the raincoat! Picton goes into the bedroom again on Saturday night. He doesn't relish seeing Elliott there on the bed with the knife sticking out of his back. He picks up something, anything, a raincoat from behind the bedroom door, he drops it over Elliott. He knows the coat can't incriminate him, it's something belonging to Elliott himself, something he kept on his premises, in the bedroom.'

Mrs Cutler lived in an old stone dwelling that had once been a farm cottage. It stood a short distance outside Littlebourne village, in a narrow rutted lane that now led nowhere.

The sun was sinking and the air turning chilly as Kelsey and Lambert walked up the path to the front door. Lambert raised the knocker and gave a couple of rat-tats.

Inside the cottage Mrs Cutler was bustling about, preparing with controlled speed for her evening's television entertainment. She had it all mapped out from the early evening news to the final good-night.

She was busy assembling her supper on a tray so that she could rush from her living-room into the kitchen at a suitable break, snatch up the tray and return to her warm nest with not a moment lost. She had already switched on the set, an old black and white, given to sulks and capricious behaviour.

She clicked her tongue in irritation when she heard the knock at the door. 'Who can that be?' she said aloud. 'Calling at this hour.' She went frowning off into the tiny hall.

'Yes?' She opened the door a fraction and peered round it with a face long practised in discouraging chance visitors.

'Good evening,' Kelsey said in a briskly cheerful voice. 'Would you mind if we stepped inside for a moment?'

She kept a tight grip on the door, didn't allow it to budge an inch. 'Have you found out who did it then?' she said challengingly. 'Have you caught him?'

Kelsey made a regretful inclination of his head. 'I'm afraid not. But one or two little matters have come up, we'd value your opinion on them.' He gave her an open, trusting smile.

She still didn't budge. 'This is a fine time to choose,' she said. 'If it's nothing important.'

'We won't keep you long.'

She flashed him a look, hearing the iron behind his wheedling tone. 'Very well then.' She knew when she'd met her match. She held the door back for them to enter, stood watching with pursed lips to make sure they wiped their feet.

'I'm very busy,' she said as she went rapidly back into the kitchen, leaving Lambert to close the front door. 'I can't spare you more than a couple of minutes.'

The hall was dark with an unmistakable smell of age. 'You're going out?' Kelsey said as he followed Mrs Cutler into the kitchen.

'I am not!' she retorted with energy. She snatched up a tin of sardines and inserted the key; she began to lever it open swiftly and expertly. 'Say what you have to say!' she said sharply. She emptied the sardines on to a small plate, covered it with a saucer and put it on the tray. 'It's the news in a couple of minutes,' she said in tones of exasperation. 'I never miss the news. Then I'm switching over to the other channel, it's a Deanna Durbin film, she's one of my favourites, I saw all her pictures when I was a girl.'

'You don't go out in the evening?' Kelsey asked. 'To the pub or bingo?'

'I do not,' she answered with contempt. 'Waste of money.' She crossed to a larder opening off the kitchen and came back with a loaf of bread on a wooden board. She plonked the board down on the table and cut several slices of bread with great rapidity. 'I don't believe in all this socializing, only leads to quarrels and bad blood.' She buttered the bread with fierce movements, slapped the slices on to a plate, covered them with another plate and put them on the tray beside the sardines. 'Anyway I don't know the locals all that well. I'm not from these parts. I came here five years ago.'

'You get on with the neighbours, though?' Kelsey said amiably. 'You stop and have a chat, drop in for a cup of tea.'

'Neighbours?' she echoed. 'What neighbours? The nearest is a good five minutes' walk. I pass the time of day if I meet anyone, no one can say I'm not civil. But that's as far as it goes.' She took the loaf back to the larder and returned carrying an old biscuit tin. She opened it and took out a massive homemade fruit cake, its top studded with incinerated raisins. She cut herself two hefty slices, then replaced the cake in the tin and carried it back to the larder. I imagine a person could fall down dead from hunger at her feet, Lambert thought, before it would cross her mind to offer so much as a crumb.

'The Pictons,' Kelsey said. 'I dare say you've come across Mrs Picton once or twice?' She gave a single nod. 'She and her husband get on all right as far as you know?'

She moved her shoulders. 'As far as I know—for what that's worth.'

'Do they strike you as a very close couple? Very united?'
She pulled a face. 'Never given it any thought.'

'Give it some thought now. Do you think Mrs Picton
would go along with everything her husband said or did
or wanted?' The Pictons had seemed to him at first a very
tight family unit, mutually supportive; now he saw them
as individuals yoked together, each separate and self-
contained.

Mrs Cutler inverted a tumbler on the tray and set
beside it a can of stout. 'I imagine she'd go along with
him—provided it suited her.'

'No more than that?'

She pulled down the corners of her mouth. 'I should
think she's got a mind of her own, quiet as she is.'

'Do you know of any lady friend Mr Elliott may have
had some little time ago, say last autumn, someone he
wasn't anxious for folk to know about?'

'If that was the case, then I'd hardly be likely to know
about it either. No, I don't know about any such lady
friend. Nor do I want to know.' She suddenly darted out
of the room, across the hall and into the living-room
opposite. Kelsey followed her. The living-room was warm
and cosy, with a coal fire burning brightly in the grate.
Near the hearth was an old, comfortable-looking wing
chair with a number of soft cushions; a leather pouffé
stood in front of it, with a checked knee-rug folded on
top. On a little table beside the chair lay a spectacle case,
some knitting, a small box of chocolates and a couple of
women's magazines. Mrs Cutler was bending over a television set standing in a corner, stabbing at the knobs.

'I've missed the news,' she said in a tone of lively complaint. A young girl appeared on the screen, smiling and
singing, a clear golden run of notes. 'What else did you
want to ask me?' Mrs Cutler demanded above the swoops
and trills. 'I do wish you'd be quick about it.'

'If you could turn the sound off for a moment,' Kelsey

said. 'We've almost finished.' She stabbed again. In the sudden silence he said, 'Young Emily Picton, have you seen much of her?'

'A good deal more than I want to.' She kept her eyes fixed on the screen where the girl was now mutely laughing and chatting, dispensing unflagging impish charm to a group of elderly men who gazed back at her in fond adoration. 'She comes sneaking into the Eastwood garden. She's a proper little madam, does exactly as she pleases, a regular little slyboots. Her parents don't know the half of it.'

'Would you call her a truthful child?'

She flashed him an astonished glance and gave a brief snorting laugh. 'That I would not. She says whatever suits her, whatever comes into her head.'

'Would you say she lived in a world of fantasy?'

'Not to put too fine a point on it, I'd say she's a natural-born liar.'

Kelsey gazed at her reflectively. Even natural-born liars might conceivably tell the truth on occasions.

Mrs Cutler leaned suddenly forward and turned the sound up again. A girlish laugh trilled out. Kelsey looked at his watch. Time they were getting back to the station anyway. 'We'll get off and leave you in peace,' he told her.

'One thing,' he said to Lambert as they walked down the path to the gate, 'I can't see Mrs Cutler dropping a word, intentional or otherwise, to any potential burglar. He'd be lucky to get the time of day from her, let alone a list of Gavin Elliott's treasures.'

Lambert opened the car door. Kelsey got in and sat looking out at the hawthorn bursting into tender cloudy green along the hedgerow. Lambert recognized that inward look; he knew better than to talk. In silence he switched on the ignition, in silence depressed the clutch.

Kelsey continued to stare ahead as the car moved off.

Such fingerprints of Leonard Picton's as they had come across at Eastwood could all be explained by the fact that it was Picton who had found the body and phoned the police. Nor were there any prints of Howard Elliott's in any situation that must necessarily raise suspicion. There were some prints of Judith Elliott's, in the sitting-room and in Elliott's bedroom, on the edge of the dressing-table mirror. She had told them—and Mrs Cutler had confirmed what she said—that she had called at Eastwood one morning some ten days before Elliott's death, to return a book she had borrowed. Mrs Cutler was alone in the house at the time, cleaning, as usual. Judith had put the book back in the sitting-room and then gone upstairs to tidy her hair in the main bedroom; it was a wild, blustery morning.

Kelsey came out of his trance. 'We'll go over to see Mrs Fiske tomorrow,' he said. 'Judith Elliott's godmother.'

Lambert said on a hesitant note, 'I suppose it isn't poss-ible that Gavin Elliott's lady friend could have been Judith Elliott?'

'I'd hardly think so,' Kelsey said after a moment. 'By all accounts Gavin was anxious to heal the family breach. He'd scarcely set about it by seducing his sister-in-law.'

'It might not have been Gavin who did the seducing. I should think Madame Judith is perfectly capable of taking the initiative herself.'

Mrs Fiske lived in a Jacobean manor house in a village some sixty miles north of Cannonbridge. She was looked after by an Italian couple who occupied a flat over the garage block—converted from the old stables.

The husband was working in the garden when they arrived. He abandoned his task and came over to them, a middle-aged man with a courteous manner and an intelli-gent eye. Kelsey saw that he knew them at once for police-men.

Yes, the Signora was at home. He conducted them to the front door where they were admitted by his wife. He said something to her in Italian and then went back to his gardening.

His wife looked at them with wariness and reserve, a shrewd peasant face, missing nothing. If the gentlemen would wait she would speak to the Signora. Kelsey stood glancing about the hall, finely panelled in oak with a superb staircase rising out of it.

She returned after a minute or two to say the Signora would see them. She showed them into a sitting-room, beautifully furnished, immaculately cared for, everything in keeping with the period of the house.

Mrs Fiske stood up from a writing-table; a fluffy little woman, still determinedly pretty — and making a fair job of it, in Lambert's opinion. He studied her unobtrusively while Kelsey explained their errand. A facelift, he judged, done by a topnotch surgeon. Her hair was a soft silvery blonde, thick and curly, skilfully arranged. After careful pondering he still couldn't decide if it was her own — or an extremely good, extremely expensive wig.

He suddenly came out of his thoughts with the realization that he was staring at her. He transferred his gaze to a handsome court cupboard standing against the opposite wall. 'A straightforward matter of confirming statements,' the Chief was saying in his most urbane tone. 'It all has to be checked, however trivial.'

'Yes, of course,' Mrs Fiske said. 'I quite understand. An appalling business. Judith told me about it over the phone. She was very upset.' She offered them refreshments and Kelsey accepted coffee.

He asked if she had known Gavin Elliott. She shook her head. 'I never had occasion to meet him. Judith told me about the family split when she got engaged to Howard, but it hadn't been made up by the time she was married, so Gavin wasn't at the wedding.'

Yes, Judith had spent a few days with her last week. Howard had joined them at the weekend. Mrs Fiske's account squared with what Kelsey had already been told. 'Howard rang Judith here about six o'clock on Friday evening,' she said. 'To say he was tired, he wouldn't be coming till next day.' She gave a sudden mischievous grin. 'I was just as pleased, I find him a trifle heavy in the hand.'

'You get on all right with him?'

'Oh yes, we don't see all that much of each other.' She grinned again. 'That helps a lot. Judith usually comes over on her own, Howard would much sooner be at one of his clubs. But it was my seventieth birthday, so he came in honour of the occasion.'

'Did Judith drive over?'

'Yes, she has her own car. Of course it meant having to drive two cars back on Sunday evening but they didn't mind that.'

'What time did Howard get here?'

'About eight o'clock on Saturday morning. Unearthly hour to arrive, he must have set off at the crack of dawn. I was just beginning to think about getting up. I said to Judith, if he was as tired as all that, why didn't he have a lie-in?'

'Perhaps he thought he'd give you a hand with the preparations for the dinner-party,' Kelsey said.

She laughed. 'I must say I'd like to see that, it would be a sight worth watching. No, he shut himself away with the newspapers while the rest of us got on with the work.'

She drank her coffee. 'But I must say I was very pleased when Judith got engaged to Howard. I was really getting rather worried about her, she never seemed to attract the right sort of man, never any substance to them. She seemed to have a positive genius for getting herself into relationships with no future. And it wasn't as if she was one of these girls with brains who can make a good career.

All she had was a dull little office job.' She gestured with a hand. 'And then, out of the blue, up pops Howard. In no time at all he was asking her to marry him. She came over here to ask my advice. I told her: Snap him up, my dear, and thank your lucky stars, you'll never get a better offer. After all, what is romance? A lot of fuss about nothing. It doesn't last; it certainly doesn't butter your bread. Security, that's the main thing, that's what counts.'

She gave a pleased little smile. 'It's turned out very well, I'm happy to say. And she's improved so much in her looks. It's having the time and money to spend on herself, it makes all the difference.'

On Saturday morning Chief-Inspector Kelsey came into his office from the canteen where he'd been having a cup of coffee with a young detective-constable who attended evening classes at the Cannonbridge College of Further Education. The constable hadn't come across Leonard Picton at the college but at Kelsey's request he'd made discreet—very discreet—inquiries among the students. 'As far as I can make out,' he told the Chief over the coffee, 'Picton's keeping his nose clean.' He wasn't much liked by the students but they respected him as a good teacher who knew his stuff and never came to class without thorough preparation. He tolerated no slackness, no larking about or casual attitudes—but he certainly didn't create scenes or hurl books around.

As to how he got on with the rest of the staff—the constable was on friendly terms with a girl in the Registrar's office; he'd gathered from her that Picton performed his duties well, kept a low profile in the college generally, joined in no activities his contract didn't oblige him to, and didn't appear to have evoked open hostility from any quarter.

Kelsey dropped into his chair and leaned forward with

his eyes closed, his elbows on the desk, his forehead resting on his clenched fists. The house-to-house inquiries in Littlebourne village had turned up no fresh lead, nor had anything of value been learned at any of the clubs and associations Elliott had belonged to. The list of missing articles had been widely circulated, without result; inquiries about the knife and raincoat had produced nothing useful. The investigations into the books and files of Elliott Gilmore had uncovered nothing in any way amiss at any of the three branches, no hint of any kind of motive for the crime.

He stood up and began to pace about the room, frowning, biting his lip. He crossed over to the window and stood looking down at the forecourt, cars arriving and leaving, a driver taking out a washleather, rubbing it over his windscreen. Fingerprints, he thought suddenly, we still haven't cleared up all the prints.

He went back to his desk and picked up a file; he began to look through the pages. There was a knock at the door and Sergeant Lambert came in. He saw the Chief's corrugated frown and set down his bundle of papers without speaking.

Kelsey stabbed a finger at a page in the file. 'Charlotte Neale,' he said. 'We haven't got her prints.' Charlotte wasn't due back from Switzerland for another week. 'And Roche's wife, we haven't got hers either. She must have gone to Eastwood with her husband a time or two.' He looked at his watch. 'We'll get over there now.' He slapped the file shut.

Roche was busy in his garden, spraying water over recently planted shrubs and roses. He turned his head at the sound of their approach and called out a greeting. 'My wife's the head gardener by rights,' he said as they came up to him. 'But it all falls to me at present. Do me good, a bit more exercise.'

'It's your wife we've come to see,' Kelsey told him.

'Oh?' Roche's head came round. Kelsey explained about the fingerprints. 'Yes, she did go with me to Eastwood once or twice,' Roche said. 'But the last time was several weeks ago. It was early in the New Year.'

'Still got to be done,' Kelsey said. 'Elimination is as useful as anything else.'

'Yes, of course. I'm not arguing, it's just that my wife isn't here at present. I'm sorry, I thought you knew.'

'No,' Kelsey said. 'I didn't know.'

'She's over at her mother's—Mrs Sparrey. She lives about ten miles from here, over Martleigh way. Annette's been rather ill, her mother's nursing her.'

'I'm sorry to hear that,' Kelsey said. 'I hope she's improving?'

'Yes, she's over the worst. I've just come from there. She's looking a lot better but the doctor wants to keep her in bed for another day or two. She had us really worried there for a while.'

'Any objection if we just called in?' Kelsey said. 'We wouldn't tire her, it wouldn't take five minutes.'

'I don't see why not.' Roche gave them the address.

'Do you see much of Howard Elliott—outside work?' Kelsey asked as he put his notebook away.

'No, not a great deal.'

'Then I don't suppose you know his wife well?'

'No, I don't.'

'Is your wife friendly with her?'

'They scarcely know each other.'

'Right then,' Kelsey said. 'We won't keep you any longer. Thanks for your help. We'll pop along now and see your wife.'

'How are things going?' Roche asked. 'Are you making any progress?'

Kelsey moved his shoulders. 'No spectacular develop-

ments. Just a slow steady slog, that's what gets results in
the end.'

Mrs Sparrey's house stood on the edge of open country, a
small semi-detached dwelling at the entrance to an unmade
road. The front garden was laid out with care, a feeling
for artistic effect.

Mrs Sparrey answered their ring at the door. A striking-
looking woman, handsome enough now at—what? Fifty-
seven or -eight? She must have been a knock-out in her
youth, Kelsey thought, unable for a moment to take his
eyes off her. She was tall and very slender with an olive
skin, eyes of so dark a brown as to appear almost black,
delicate winged brows, steel-grey hair thick and smooth,
swept back from her finely-sculptured face in a gleaming
roll. She wore a shirt tucked into slacks, and a sleeveless
pullover, all in shades of grey and brown; the only splash
of colour was her russet lipstick.

She didn't seem surprised or put out by their appearance on her doorstep—but of course Roche would have
rung to tell her they were on their way. Her manner was
poised and assured; it would probably take a great deal to
throw her out of her stride.

Kelsey explained their errand. 'Yes, of course,' she said
at once. Her tone was friendly and cooperative. She stood
aside for them to enter. 'What a terrible business,' she
said as she closed the door.

'Were you ever in Eastwood yourself?' Kelsey asked.

'No, I never even met the poor young man. I'll just tell
my daughter you're here.' She left them in the sitting-
room while she went upstairs.

Kelsey glanced round the room, comfortable, furnished
with taste, no great expenditure of money, but some
highly individual touches. To the right of the hearth a
cabinet displaying a collection of old ruby glass, full of
glow and light. On one wall a number of framed photo-

graphs and playbills, skilfully arranged. He crossed the room and studied them. The largest photograph showed a troupe of showgirls in full rig, plumes, sequins, jewelled breastplates. In smaller photographs the same girls, in more conventional dress, appeared at receptions, parades, in the foyers of theatres and restaurants. The playbills were from large towns and cities scattered across Europe.

It didn't take Kelsey long to pick out Mrs Sparrey from among the spangled charmers. 'She was certainly a looker,' he said to Lambert. He turned at the sound of steps on the stairs. Mrs Sparrey came into the room. She still had the dancer's beautiful carriage and grace of movement.

'You can go up now,' she told them. 'It's the door on the right.' Her smile, the movements of her head and hands, all clearly displayed the enduring results of training but without theatricality or conscious striving for effect.

Annette Roche's bedroom was small but charmingly furnished. Venetian blinds filtered the pale sunlight; a bowl of freesias scented the air with a light delicate fragrance. Annette was sitting up in bed, leaning back into a nest of lacy pillows. She looked tired and wan but she smiled at them as they came in.

If Kelsey was expecting a younger version of Mrs Sparrey he was disappointed; he could see no resemblance between mother and daughter. Annette's skin was fair and her hair chestnut; her eyes were grey with long dark lashes. He put her at around twenty-seven.

'I hope it hasn't been very inconvenient for you,' she said. 'Having to come over especially to see me.' Her voice was low but clear. She smiled again; she had pretty, pearly teeth, small and even.

'It's no trouble,' Kelsey said. 'I take it your mother's explained about the fingerprints. If you'd allow Sergeant Lambert . . .'

While Lambert was busy Kelsey asked if she could recall when she had last visited Eastwood. She frowned a little. 'I think the last time was in January—yes, that's right, early in January.' Elliott had asked them to dinner at the Caprice, a seasonal gesture of hospitality. Howard and Judith Elliott were there, together with a couple of business associates and their wives. They had all gone along to Eastwood afterwards for a drink, had spent an hour or so there. She had never been in the house since, had never been there at any time on her own, had never had occasion to call in uninvited.

Kelsey asked if she knew anything that might be of any interest to them in the case but she shook her head. She had scarcely known Elliott, knew nothing of his private life. She drew a long, trembling sigh. 'I could hardly credit it when Stephen told me, I couldn't take it in. I was feeling so ill myself at the time, it was like part of some feverish nightmare.' She had been feeling unwell for some days, had begun to feel really ill as the week progressed but had hung on, thinking she would give in and go to bed as soon as her husband got home on Friday evening.

'But then he rang to say he had to go to a dinner, so he would be staying the night in Martleigh, he had to go into the office on Saturday morning.' She had told him it was just as well, she wasn't feeling too good, she'd go over to her mother's and let her nurse her. She had put a few things in her car and driven over, had gone straight to bed and been there ever since. 'And very glad to be here,' she added. 'I felt pretty rotten for a few days.' She gave the Chief a direct, unsmiling look and all at once a thought stabbed at him: That face, that look. I've seen her before.

The thought niggled at him during the remaining minute or two they were in the room. Nothing about her he could place; the tone of her voice, her smile, colouring, mannerisms, none of these could he recognize. And yet the thought persisted.

Could it have been her photograph he'd seen? But they hadn't been inside Greenlawn and he couldn't recall any photograph of her in Roche's office, or in any of the other premises they'd visited in the course of the case.

'I've a notion I've seen her before somewhere,' he said to Lambert as they got into the car again and headed back towards Cannonbridge. He drew his brows together, trying to snare the elusive recollection.

'I certainly don't know her face,' Lambert said. 'Perhaps she reminds you of someone you've seen on TV. I spent half a day once trying to remember where I'd seen someone. I was sure he was a right villain, I kept getting this association with armed hold-ups.' He'd solved the mystery a week or two later, watching a Western one evening on television. 'He was the spitting image of that chap who always played the part of the manager of a small-town bank. The one that always tries to be brave when the stick-up starts and always ends up getting shot.'

Kelsey leaned back and closed his eyes; he felt all at once unutterably weary. By the time they reached Cannonbridge he had fallen into an uneasy sleep. Lambert halted the car on the forecourt of the police station. He put a hand on the Chief's arm. Kelsey woke on the instant, sitting up with a violent start. He stayed in the car for a minute or two, yawning and rubbing his eyes, then he got out and walked over to the steps. The moment he went in through the swing doors the tide of work rose to engulf him again.

Saturday came to an end at last. Sunday would be another working day, with luck a shade less frenetic.

It was nearly eight when Kelsey let himself into his flat not far from the police station. He lived alone now, had done so for a year or two. He'd been married once but it hadn't jelled; right from the start she'd resented the demands of the Force. After the divorce he'd tried living in lodgings, tried sharing a house with an older, widowed sister, but in the end he'd settled for this flat on his own. Lonely sometimes, but he could come and go as he pleased, his erratic hours disturbed no one; no one sat up watching the clock, worrying if he was late. He had only his own moods and bouts of ill temper to cope with.

He'd got a routine of sorts going and it worked tolerably well. One of the station cleaners came in a couple of mornings a week to run a duster over the place and take his stuff to the laundrette. He ate in the station canteen or in a cheap café; he had chronic indigestion.

Now he settled down to watch television, but the long days were beginning to catch up with him. By half past nine the nerves and muscles in the calves of his legs were starting to twitch and jump, always a sign that he'd better call it quits. He was in bed by ten and dropped at once into a dark and dreamless abyss.

At seven in the morning when the alarm shrilled beside his bed he opened his eyes and at once sat bolt upright on the sudden flaring thought: Kingsharbour! That's where I saw her! She's Mrs M!

Exhilaration ran through his veins. He sprang out of bed and began with speed and energy to prepare for the day ahead.

When Lambert came into the station, still yawning after a restless night and a hasty breakfast, he found the Chief on the phone in his office; he had already been at work for the best part of an hour. The Chief finished his call, tilted back his chair and looked at Lambert with a bright, vigorous eye full of glinting energy.

'I've just been on to Kingsharbour,' he said. 'Fixing us up a nice little trip to the seaside. Tomorrow morning, crack of dawn.' Lambert said nothing, resigned by now to anything the Chief might suddenly decide on in the course of an investigation—Timbuctoo or the North Pole.

Kelsey linked his hands behind his head and smiled like a man who enjoys every moment of a full existence. 'I remembered where I'd seen Annette Roche,' he said with deep pleasure. 'It was five years ago, I was down south when my aunt was in hospital, when she was dying. I saw Annette's photograph in the local paper. Of course she wasn't Annette Roche then, she was married to some Pole with an unpronounceable name, the papers called her Mrs M.'

'Means nothing to me,' Lambert said.

'It never made the nationals, it wasn't a particularly interesting case. I didn't bother to follow it—and anyway I'd other things on my mind. I couldn't get anyone who'd worked on the case when I phoned just now but I did find out what happened to her. She got off.'

'Got off from what?'

'She killed her husband. No question about it, she freely admitted it. The question was whether it was murder. It seems the jury decided it wasn't.' He banged down the legs of his chair. 'Do you know how she killed him? How she admitted killing him?' He jabbed at the air with a forefinger. 'She ran him through the heart with a breadknife.'

CHAPTER 11

'I was very fond of my aunt,' Kelsey said. 'I used to go down and spend three or four weeks with her in the summer holidays when I was a lad. She had a cottage a few miles from Kingsharbour.' Five years ago his aunt had suffered a stroke and been taken to hospital; he immediately took his annual leave in order to be with her.

By the time she died he had spent a good deal of time hanging about the hospital corridors and canteen; he had picked up and glanced at a good many discarded newspapers, hardly taking in the contents.

And one day looking back at him from a newspaper, direct and unsmiling, had been the face of Mrs M.

'From what I remember,' he said, 'her husband was a seaman, the son of a wartime refugee. He came home after one trip and accused her of being up to no good while he was away. There was a quarrel, a fight, she picked up a knife to defend herself.'

Kingsharbour had told him that the superintendent in charge of the case was retired now, was at present on a protracted visit to his married daughter in New Zealand. There was an inspector at the station who had worked on the case as a sergeant. He was off duty when Kelsey phoned, but he would be in the station tomorrow morning.

He began to whistle on a single note, jerky little spurts of sound. 'I'll have to be back here again by tomorrow night,' he said to Lambert. 'But you can stay on another day if it seems to warrant it. I can always come back by train.'

The final stretch of the road to Kingsharbour lay across a flat expanse of heath, bleak and barren-looking, dotted with firs and pine trees.

The harbour was of medium size, with dry docks, the remains of town walls and ancient fortifications; a newer township had been grafted on to the old port.

It was getting on for half past ten as Lambert drove Kelsey out to the comparatively modern suburb where the couple had lived, towards the police station that had handled the case.

'Miszowski,' the Inspector said. 'Bit of a mouthful. You

can see why the press cut it down to Mrs M.' He inclined his head. 'The Super was more than half inclined to believe her story. There's no doubt she was an attractive young woman, she had a way of walking, a long, narrow waist.' He gave a small, reminiscent smile. 'The Super wouldn't have believed her tale for two minutes together if she'd been fat and cross-eyed.'

'And what was her tale?' Kelsey asked.

'She said her husband knocked her about. He would come home from his ship, everything would be fine for a day or two, then he'd start drinking, get among his pals at the pub, come home drunk and start asking her what she'd been up to while he was away, start thumping her. According to her she'd never been up to anything. He was as right as ninepence when he was sober but with the drink inside him it was always jealousy and suspicions. On this particular evening she'd laid the table for supper. He came in, started yelling at her right away, accusing her. She had the knife in her hand purely by chance, she was cutting bread when he came charging in. She thrust up her hand to defend herself, he went straight on to the knife.'

'Sounds possible,' Kelsey said. 'Did you believe her?'

'I did not. It was mainly a look she had, I can't quite put a word to it, a sort of aware, slightly calculating look. She put up a first-class performance in court, I'll give her that. Neat dark suit, white blouse, hair smarmed back, no make-up, downcast eyes, low voice. I half expected the judge to give her a pound out of the poorbox.'

'What do you think actually happened?'

'My belief is that her husband was a decent enough chap, quiet, hardworking, fond of her. I never saw any hard evidence to suggest otherwise. There were two main witnesses to say he was in the habit of drinking too much and getting stroppy. One of them was an old shipmate of his, but I didn't like the look of him, I wouldn't have staked tuppence on his honesty.'

'And the other witness?'

'The other witness was her mother. Mrs Sparrey.'

Kelsey sat up.

'Mrs Sparrey went into the box,' the Inspector said. 'She swore black and blue Miszowski used to knock her daughter about, that she'd known about it for some time, Annette had come to her with bruises and so on. She'd advised her to leave him. She'd tried to talk to the husband, but he was as meek as water when he was sober, would promise anything. Everything would go along swimmingly—till the next time. Annette had told her she didn't want to leave him, she still loved him. All she wanted was for him to mend his ways, she was sure it would turn out all right in the end.' He paused and then added, 'There's no doubt about it, Miszowski was drunk at the time he was stabbed, the post mortem showed that beyond question.'

'It could have been the way she told it,' Kelsey said. He'd come across many a man who was one thing in his cups and quite another stone cold sober.

The Inspector grinned. 'You won't convince me,' he said with a shake of his head. 'But she convinced the jury all right, she had them eating out of her hand. And Mrs Sparrey told the tale well in court. A real head-turner, she was. She kept a café in the town, down by the harbour, a very well run place, never any trouble. Trudi's, it was called. She upped sticks and left after the case. I don't know where she went to.'

'I do,' Kelsey said. 'She's living near her daughter, about ten miles out of Cannonbridge.'

'Is that so?' The Inspector pulled down the corners of his mouth. 'They struck me as very close. Annette used to work in the café before she was married—she married very young, barely eighteen. Her mother was against the marriage, she wanted something better for her daughter.

She never let her wait at table, she put her in a little cashier's office, dressed up like a lady. One of the young constables we had here at that time, he was absolutely potty about Annette Sparrey. He spent every spare moment and every penny of his pay on cups of coffee and doughnuts at Trudi's, just so he could gaze on Annette. Poor sod, he was always covered in pimples and boils.'

'Are you saying Mrs Sparrey lied in court to save her daughter?'

'That's exactly what I'm saying. I've no proof of it, not even a glimmer of a shadow of proof, but I'm quite certain of it. She put up a lovely performance, they were a talented pair of actresses. And Annette's counsel—he painted this heart-rending picture of an innocent girl and her suffering mother, this violent, drunken beast of a husband, I nearly wept myself when I heard him. I don't know whether he believed she was innocent or guilty, she ran rings round all of them. And her solicitor, he worked like a beaver on the case—afterwards of course it was clear why.'

'Why was that?'

'She married him.'

'Married him?' Kelsey echoed. 'What was his name?' He felt the hair prickle along his scalp.

'Roche. Stephen Roche. They were married after the trial. Roche resigned from his job—with a local firm of solicitors—and he and Annette vanished from Kingsharbour.'

CHAPTER 12

Kelsey looked at the Inspector in silence, then he said, 'Are you suggesting that Miszowski's death was deliberate murder? Planned and executed in cold blood?'

'I am. I'm suggesting that Annette regularly used to get up to mischief when her husband was away and that she'd been getting away with it, her husband was none the wiser. I believe he did take a drink and he did come home fairly plastered from time to time when he was on leave, but I believe that was as far as it went. I don't believe he ever laid a finger on Annette; he just fell asleep or got maudlin or amorous when he'd had a few. I think on this occasion someone wrote to him while he was away at sea, or else he heard from some kind well-wisher the moment he set foot in a pub ashore, that his wife had been playing around. I believe there was an almighty row and he threatened to throw her out.

'That didn't suit Madame Annette. She had a little think and decided she'd had enough of being married to Miszowski, she could do a great deal better elsewhere. But she had no intention of leaving empty-handed. She intended to get the house, the furniture, the car, and whatever money he had.

'So the next time Miszowski came lurching in from the pub she'd set the scene, she'd laid the table with a bread-knife handy. Miszowski came staggering in, half seas over. She simply went up to him and ran the knife up under his ribs. Or else she waited till he'd dropped into a chair, leaned back and closed his eyes, begun to snore. She knelt down in front of him and stuck the knife in, took her time about it, got it right. I suggest she went to some trouble beforehand to find out exactly what spot would be best. He jerked his head. 'I believe she did it in cold blood. That single, sure knife thrust, clinical and cold-blooded, to my mind that's the mark of a real killer.'

The Inspector linked his hands behind his head and tilted back his chair. 'Mrs Sparrey arrived on the scene a few minutes after we got there. Annette was distraught. the place was a bit of a shambles. Annette told us that as soon as she realized Miszowski was dead she rang the

police and then phoned her mother. But I believe she did
one or two little jobs before she rang the police, such as
smashing the place up a bit, giving herself a couple of
bruises. Then she rang her mother and they concocted a
story between them. And then, finally, Annette rang us.'

'Are you suggesting that she planned the whole thing
beforehand with her mother?'

'No, not at all. I believe she did plan the whole thing,
but on her own. She only brought her mother into it when
it was all over and Miszowski was dead. I'm sure she told
her mother a plausible tale and her mother believed her:
how Miszowski had come in drunk, picked a quarrel,
gone to attack her and she'd lashed out with a knife she
had by chance in her hand. She probably threw herself on
her mother's mercy, said something like: They'll never
believe it was an accident — but if I tell them he'd been in
the habit of knocking me about, and if you back me up in
that, then they'll believe me.'

The Inspector banged down the legs of his chair. 'I
fancy that was about the size of it. Mrs Sparrey was very
fond of her daughter. I don't suppose it crossed her mind
it could all be a put-up job, she'd never believe such a
thing of her darling. I'm sure she did genuinely believe it
was an accident. If it was just a question of a few white
lies to protect her daughter, then I'm certain she could be
relied on for that. All in good faith, all with the best of
intentions.' He looked at Kelsey. 'What's this case you're
on now?'

'The murder of a young man,' Kelsey said. 'A good-
looking young man, stabbed to death, asleep in his bed.'

The Inspector put the tips of his fingers together. 'And
Annette Roche is somewhere in the picture?'

'It's possible.'

The Inspector began to whistle soundlessly. 'Where
does she say she was when he was killed?'

'Ill in bed at her mother's house. She says she'd been

there for some hours before the death. She's still there now.'

The Inspector laughed. 'Of course she is. Where else would she be? Where better? Mrs Sparrey will guard her like a bulldog till it's all over. And Roche—he'll lie his head off for her.'

'But he's not her solicitor now,' Kelsey said. 'He's her husband. If she killed Elliott, the implication must surely be that she was having an affair with him: there was some kind of quarrel between them, perhaps he got cold feet and wanted to break it off, perhaps he found someone else and she killed him in a fit of jealousy. Surely Roche wouldn't cover up for her if that was the case?'

The Inspector made a dismissive gesture. 'That wouldn't be the story she'd tell Roche. She'd spin him some yarn he could swallow. He was absolutely nuts about her, he gave up a first-class legal career for her. She'd tell him she'd been tricked, seduced, anything, she wanted to end it but he wouldn't let her, she lost her head—any kind of tomfool tale. You must have come across dozens of men who've swallowed cock and bull stories from women they were mad about.'

Kelsey had come across them all right—and women too, who'd believed outrageous lies from husbands and lovers, tales that were an insult to judgment and common sense.

'Roche had got her out of one nasty hole,' the Inspector said. 'Habit would impel him to get her out of another.' He never ceased to be amazed at the way in which sane and sober citizens went on pulling chestnuts out of the fire for wilfully irresponsible dependants and associates; the records of criminal history were full of such cases.

'Roche worked for a firm called Amphlett and Watson,' he said. 'By far the best firm round here. You could go along and have a word with Osborne, he was their managing clerk till he retired a couple of years ago.

*

Osborne was a bachelor, a lean, sinewy, gimlet-eyed man with pepper-and-salt hair and shoulders much stooped from years of sitting at a desk. He was at home in his flat on the ground floor of an Edwardian house in a residential suburb in the old part of Kingsharbour. He had just finished clearing away his meagre lunch and was about to take his walk to a neighbouring park, when the two men walked up the front path.

But he was by no means put out by this disruption of his routine. He received them with lively interest. 'Come in, come in,' he said when Kelsey had indicated his errand. He showed them into a room overflowing with books and papers. 'Do sit down.' He waved a hand. 'If you can find anywhere.' He swept books and papers from the seats of chairs on to the floor. 'Living alone,' he said airily, 'one gets into sad habits.' The room was thickly filmed with dust, the carpet was dotted with curls of fluff.

'Oh yes, I remember the case all right,' Osborne said when they were all at last seated in varying degrees of discomfort. 'It created a tremendous stir at Amphlett and Watson, Roche leaving like that.' His eyes sparkled with pleasure. 'It was a lively time in the old firm just then, I can tell you.'

'I gather Roche resigned when the trial was over,' Kelsey said.

'Resigned would be one way of putting it,' Osborne said with the same malicious edge to his tone. 'He didn't have much option. Old Amphlett—he's still there, getting on for eighty now but still puts in a day's work, he'll live to be a hundred, I shouldn't wonder—Amphlett was outraged by the whole affair, he was livid with Roche.' He smiled, savouring the recollection. 'He was particularly incensed because he'd got Roche lined up for a partnership before all this blew up. He had a very high opinion of Roche's legal ability. Of course he'd known Roche's father for donkey's years, the judge—'

'Judge?' Kelsey said.

'Yes, Neville Roche, circuit judge in this area, very well known and respected, very upright man, very high-principled. Retired now, he's bought a pretty little cottage.' He mentioned a village a few miles from Kingsharbour. 'He took it very hard when his son married Mrs M. and left Amphlett and Watson. It was a terrible blow to him, but he wouldn't show it openly; he'd be crucified before he let anyone see how much it shook him. He finished with his son completely over the affair—and Stephen was his only child.'

'What about Stephen Roche's mother?' Kelsey asked. 'How did she take all this?'

'She was in no position to take it any way at all,' Osborne said with relish. 'She'd been dead—' he screwed up his eyes—'must have been twenty years or more, when all this happened.' He leaned forward and spoke in a confidential tone. 'You know her story?'

Kelsey shook his head.

'She ran away from Neville Roche when Stephen was five or six years old. She was a very pretty woman, years younger than old Neville—he was always a dry old stick, even when he was forty. She ran off with a very good-looking young fellow—talk about Clark Gable! Roche divorced her. She didn't try to get custody of Stephen, she knew she didn't have a cat in hell's chance, different days then. Roche never even let her have any access to the boy. She married her handsome young man. I heard two or three years later that she'd died in childbirth.'

'Did Neville Roche marry again?'

'Not he. Once bitten. He was never cut out for marriage anyway. He sent Stephen off to a prep school after his wife ran off. Ryecroft, it's not far from here, the best prep school in the county. He set his heart on the lad going in for the law, following in his footsteps.'

'I'm not quite clear,' Kelsey said, 'what all the rumpus was about. It's surely not a crime to get your client off a charge of murder and then marry her.'

Osborne gave a snort of a laugh. 'Maybe not, but it's every sort of crime against legal ethics to say your client has consulted you about the violent behaviour of her husband when she did nothing of the sort.' He gave a sideways jerk of his head. 'And Amphlett had a shrewd suspicion Roche had been tampering with witnesses, or at least assisting them in the doctoring of evidence.'

Kelsey raised his eyebrows.

'It was a pretty vital question,' Osborne said. 'Had Miszowski been knocking his wife about or not? The whole case hinged on that. There was just the mother's word to back up Annette's statement. But now you have this highly respectable solicitor—and, mark you, no suggestion whatever of any extra-mural interest in his client, not a word, not a whisper, till it was all over and off to the registry office with the pair of them—here he is, solemnly stating she came to see him six months before her husband's death, asking for advice about separation or divorce on the grounds of cruelty, unreasonable behaviour and so forth.'

'You don't believe she did consult him?'

'Oh yes, she consulted him all right, but not about her husband. She had a suède coat, an expensive garment, she'd sent it to the cleaner's and they'd ruined it. She came to see Roche about that. He wrote to the cleaners a letter threatening proceedings, and they paid up. I dare say she sized Roche up at that time, saw he fancied her. He was a sitting duck as far as a woman like that was concerned: always quiet and reserved, no social life to speak of. Later, when she needed a solicitor in a hurry, someone who'd be likely to swallow her tale, she went along to Roche.' He waved a hand. 'And then there was the business of the neighbour.'

'Neighbour?'

'An elderly man, lived next door to the Miszowskis. He was a widower with a son in Australia. When he retired the son pressed him to sell up and go out to join him. The idea was he should bring out his capital and they'd buy a place between them, so of course the old man was keen to get the best price he could for his property. He put it up for sale and had several nibbles, but they always came to nothing, always for the same reason: there was no garage, no access for a car and no possibility of access.' He tilted back his head. 'Of course I didn't know all this at the time; it's what I ferreted out later, after Roche had left the firm. Anyway, the neighbour went next door and asked Miszowski if he'd sell him a strip of land adjoining his property, to make room for a garage. The Miszowskis had a good big garden, he was sure they wouldn't miss the strip. He offered them a fair price but Miszowski wouldn't sell.

'Then, a few months later, Miszowski is stabbed to death. By the time the police get round to asking the neighbour—he was the only near neighbour—if he knew anything of Mrs M's way of life, if she got up to tricks when her husband was away at sea, and so forth, Roche had already been along to see him. Roche told him Mrs M. would now be putting her own house on the market, she was willing to sell him the strip of land.' He smiled. 'Of course in order to sell it she had to be found innocent. If she was found guilty she couldn't profit by her crime, couldn't inherit the property, couldn't sell off bits of the garden. I imagine Roche made all that crystal clear.' He gave a knowing nod. 'No doubt Roche and the neighbour understood each other very well.'

'All this is of course only assumption on your part,' Kelsey observed mildly.

Osborne thrust out his lips. 'A pretty fair assumption, based on all the known facts. I made it my business to

find out what figure the land changed hands for. It was
well below market price. And when the police did get
round to talking to the neighbour he was as dumb as an
oyster, he didn't know anything, he'd never seen
anything, never heard anything, couldn't tell them
anything. Shortly after the trial was over he sold his house
for a very satisfactory figure and took himself off to
Australia.' He gave the Chief a challenging look. 'And
those are not assumptions, those are hard facts.'

There was a brief pause, then Osborne said with an air
of pleasurable anticipation, 'Why all this sudden interest
in Mrs M. now? After all this time?'

Kelsey eyed him in silence, then he gave him the barest
outline of the facts, no speculations, no deductions, a
good deal less than Osborne would have learned if he had
picked up a copy of the Cannonbridge newspaper.

Osborne began to laugh immoderately. He took out a
handkerchief and dabbed at his eyes. 'My word,' he said,
'I didn't know I was going to have such an enjoyable afternoon when I stood at the sink washing up my lunch
things.' He put his handkerchief back in his pocket. 'A
creature of impulse, our Annette, that was always her
trouble, a lady of passion.' His tone sobered somewhat.
'But you won't nail her, I'll bet you anything you like.'

'Oh, I'll have her,' Kelsey said. 'If she did it I'll have
her. So far there's not a shred of evidence against her.
Nothing to suggest she had anything to do with Elliott's
death, nothing that connects her with Elliott in the
slightest degree.'

Osborne looked at him with shrewd cold eyes totally
devoid now of mirth. 'You have a man stabbed to death,'
he said, 'and you have — what? — four or five people in his
circle who might conceivably have done it. Ask yourself
this, Chief Inspector: in any ordinary group of that size in
respectable society in an English provincial town, would
you expect to find two separate, totally unconnected

'individuals, each of them prepared at some time in their lives to stab a man to death?'

CHAPTER 13

After Lambert had dropped the Chief at the railway station on his way back to Cannonbridge, his first action was to find himself somewhere for the night. All along the seafront boarding-houses reared their stately Victorian frontages; Lambert chose the house with the cleanest curtains and the most highly polished brass knocker.

The door was opened to him by a man not far off sixty. Yes, certainly he could have a bed for the night, the house was almost empty at this time of year.

Lambert deposited his bag in the bedroom and went downstairs again. The landlord showed a strong disposition to chat, offered him tea, a cigarette, and even, as a last persuasion, something stronger than tea. But Lambert had other fish to fry.

It didn't take him long to find Trudi's down by the harbour. The café had clearly been modernized and smartened up in the last year or two. At this time of day, according to the menu, teas of various kinds were being served: Afternoon Tea, Snack Tea, High Tea, Substantial High Tea and Hungry Man's Tea. Lambert, ravenous from the salty air, chose the Hungry Man's Tea. And it certainly seemed ample enough when it arrived, brought by a cheerful-looking young woman in a print dress and frilled apron. Two poached eggs on lavishly buttered toast, a selection of appetising-looking sandwiches, toasted scones, and a plate of fancy iced cakes.

'That should stop your gallop for an hour or two,' the waitress said with a grin. He exchanged a little badinage with her. 'I haven't seen you in here before,' she said.

'Taking an early holiday?'

He nodded. 'I used to know a girl who worked here,' he said as he started on the poached eggs. He plucked a name from the air. 'I met her that last time I was down here, must be what? — four or five years ago. I wondered if she was still here.'

She laughed. 'She'll have got tired of waiting for you to show up again. There's no one of that name at Trudi's now.'

'I suppose there isn't anyone on the staff who might know where she went? I'd like to see her again.'

'Four or five years,' she said. 'It's a long time. Staff come and go in a place like this.' She pondered. 'Oh yes, Lily Yarworth, she might know. She used to work in the kitchen here, she was here for years. She's retired now, she left a few months ago.'

'You don't happen to know where she lives?'

'I do, as a matter of fact. She has a bedsit in a house not far from here, Tidworth Street, number 21.' She picked up her tray. 'Tell her to look in and see us one of the days.'

No. 21 Tidworth Street was an old terrace house in a street that was slipping into a slum. Lambert could hear a variety of sounds as he pressed the front doorbell and stood waiting: two women quarrelling in the house next door, three or four radios playing, all tuned in to different stations, a baby crying over the road, a door banging, a dog barking.

The door was jerked open and a young Negro boy ran a swiftly assessing eye over Lambert.

'Does Miss Lily Yarworth live here?' Lambert asked.

The boy nodded. 'Up the stairs, first on your right.' He darted out into the street and raced off.

Lambert stepped inside. The hall was dark and smelt of paraffin. He went up the stairs, covered with worn carpet. On the first door on the right a postcard secured with drawing-pins announced: MISS LILY YARWORTH, in neat block capitals.

His knock was answered by a small, stout woman with a good deal of white hair coiled up in loops and whorls on top of her head. She held the door wide and looked out at him with a friendly smile as if glad to see a visitor.

'Miss Yarworth?' Behind her he could see a table with an open newspaper, a pair of spectacles lying beside it, a set of bookshelves against the wall, crammed with paperbacks.

'Yes, I'm Lily Yarworth,' she said cheerfully. She stepped back. 'Do come in. I was just going to make a cup of tea.' She shuffled across to the sink and picked up a kettle. Her legs were thick and shapeless, the arches of her feet long since dropped.

'I'm writing a book,' he said as she filled the kettle. 'About the history of Kingsharbour.' She turned and gave him a look of keen interest. 'I'm including a chapter on local court cases,' he said. 'I was told you might be able to help me with one of them. It was a few years back, the name was Miszowski.'

'Oh yes,' she said at once. She smiled with pleasure. 'I knew them well. Annette and her mother.' She set the kettle on to boil. 'Go ahead, ask me anything you want to know.'

'Perhaps you could just start talking, say whatever you remember. You won't mind if I make a couple of notes. You might begin by saying how you came to know Mrs Sparrey and her daughter.'

'Yes, all right.' She took cups and saucers from a cupboard. 'Mrs Sparrey used to be a dancer,' she began. 'I met her—must be twenty-seven or -eight years ago.' She paused and made a mental calculation. 'Yes, that's right. Annette must be twenty-seven now, and I met Mrs Sparrey a few months before Annette was born.' She pulled a little face. 'Between you and me, there never was any Mr Sparrey, Sparrey was her own name, she just called herself Mrs. She'd been left in the lurch, some chap she met while she was abroad with the dancing troupe. He vanished when she told him there was a baby on the way. It was different in those days, not like it is now, they don't make a secret of it any more. She knew she'd have to give up the dancing soon, so she left the troupe and came back to England.' The kettle boiled and she made the tea. 'She'd saved quite a bit and she had a lot of jewellery, good stuff, given to her, you know, she'd always kept it for a rainy day. She sold it and took a lease on a café.'

'What made her choose Kingsharbour?'

'It was just where she happened to land up when she came back. And she wanted somewhere where she wasn't known.' She poured the tea and passed him a cup. 'She had some foreign blood in her. She was born abroad, I think it was in South Africa. She said something one New Year's Eve when we were closing, we'd both had a couple of drinks. She started talking about her own family, about when she was a kid. She'd been strictly brought up, she said she couldn't ever go back there, not with a child and no husband. They'd never wanted her to go on the stage in the first place.'

She got out a tin of biscuits and pushed them across the table to Lambert. 'The café was a run-down place. She got it very cheap and worked it up, there's plenty of trade in that part of town. Her name was Gertrude but she'd always called herself Trudi when she was dancing, so that's what she called the café, Trudi's.'

She took a biscuit and began to eat it in an abstracted fashion. 'I was working at the café when she bought it, that's how we met. She asked me to stay on when she took over. We always got on well, right from the start. She was always very straight with me and I worked hard for her, I helped her to build the business up. She was a hard worker herself, never stopped, she only took ten days off when Annette was born.' She looked up at him. 'She absolutely doted on that child.'

'And Miszowski?' Lambert asked. 'Annette's husband?'

'I always liked him. Tall, very good-looking, quiet chap. Tanned face, blue eyes and black hair. He was quite a bit older than Annette, ten or twelve years. She was only seventeen when she met him. He came into the café one day, she fell for him right away. Mrs Sparrey didn't take it very seriously at first but Annette was set on marrying him. She could be very determined, and her mother could never really stand out against her when she had her mind set on something, she was much too fond of her for that. She would never have fallen out with Annette, that girl meant more to her than anything on God's earth.' She turned her head and looked out of the window. 'Not that Mrs Sparrey had anything against him, just that she wanted something better for Annette. But when she saw she couldn't talk her out of it she put a good face on it. She gave them a nice little reception at the café.'

'Did she see much of Annette after the marriage?'

'Not a great deal. Annette was living over in the new part of town. They had a nice house over there, seven Swanpool Road.'

'Were you surprised by what happened? The way Miszowski died?'

'Surprised? I was absolutely staggered. I'd never heard a word about this quarrelling and him knocking her about.'

'After the trial, were you surprised when she married Stephen Roche?'

She poured more tea. 'I certainly was, but I thought it a very good thing for her.' She fingered a biscuit, broke it into pieces. 'A girl in her position at that time, she'd have been mad to turn him down. And Mrs Sparrey was delighted, it was the sort of match she'd always wanted for Annette. It was a very quiet wedding, a lovely spring day, the beginning of April.' She pushed the fragments of biscuit round her plate. 'I often think about them, wonder where they are, how they're getting on. Mrs Sparrey and me, we went through a lot together, good times and bad, you don't forget that. And I was very fond of Annette, I'd known her since the day she was born. November baby, she was, November the twenty-fifth. Sagittarius, that is.'

She blew out a long breath. 'Funny mixture, Sagittarians. Too trusting, easily taken in. All for excitement and pleasure, always looking for romance. They rush into things, then they're dissatisfied; they can't cope with difficulties, won't persevere, they lose their heads.' She looked up at him. 'Do you follow the stars? It's a bit of a hobby of mine.'

Lambert shook his head.

She gave him a smiling, challenging look. 'Oh, you can look like that, but I bet I can tell you your birthsign.' She tilted back her head and studied him. 'Pisces,' she said at last. 'Doesn't pay you to get your feet wet.'

Lambert's eyes jerked open. Pisces he was, and if he got his feet soaked, as sure as Christmas he'd be blowing his nose a couple of days later.

She wagged a finger at him. 'Doesn't pay to scoff. You don't know all the answers in this life, book-writer or not.'

Swanpool Road was in a pleasant enough area, tree-lined roads, orderly gardens, red-brick houses, a few shops. No. 7 was a detached house, three or four bedrooms, Lambert guessed. The garden was still a fair size even without the strip for the garage, a concrete structure set down close beside the cottage next door.

As Lambert stood looking at the two dwellings a young woman came out of the back door of the cottage, carrying a laundry basket. She went off down the garden to where a line of washing blew in the breeze. She set her basket down on the grass and began to unpeg the washing.

Lambert walked slowly off up the road, past a small public garden, a row of lock-up shops, a Nonconformist chapel. On the other side of the road was a grassy plot with an estate agent's board, a school of dancing, a large detached house hidden away behind trees.

There were two pubs fairly close to Swanpool Road, a small old neighbourhood pub in a side-street, and a larger, more modern pub on the main road. Lambert crossed the threshold of the small pub ten minutes after opening time. A few old men were already drinking their first pints; they were joined before long by other regulars, obviously equally well established, middle-aged husbands and wives, young couples, one or two elderly women.

Lambert couldn't get on terms with any of them, couldn't manage to come within a mile of striking up any conversation beyond the most banal everyday observations. After twenty minutes he abandoned the struggle and tried his luck at the second pub.

He fared no better there. A darts match was in progress, a good deal of loud laughter and jollity. In the lounge bar loving couples, in the snug a party of boisterous women arranging details of some outing. He wandered about, did his best here and there, but after another twenty minutes he gave up and went off to his car. I'll try the waterfront, he decided, without much hope.

There was no difficulty in finding a pub in the harbour area, the difficulty lay in choosing among them. He walked through the doors of the first pub he decided on at seven-fifteen and left his sixth and last pub a few minutes after the landlord called time. At none of them did he have the slightest sniff of success. In all of them they closed ranks against him, knowing him at once for what he was, recognizing his air of casual-seeming purpose, the way he made one drink last out his visit, his build and grooming, general deportment.

It was a fine clear night as he drove back to his boarding-house. The door was opened by the landlord. He gave Lambert a friendly grin as he admitted him, rolled his eyes in an upward direction and raised a finger to his lips; he closed the door carefully and silently. He jerked his head to indicate that Lambert should follow him into the sitting-room.

'We'll have a little nightcap,' he said in a more normal but still guarded tone when the sitting-room door was safely closed behind them. 'The wife's gone up to bed.' Lambert watched with feigned enthusiasm as he poured a couple of stiff whiskies.

'Cheers!' The landlord raised his glass. 'Dead as the tomb round here before the season starts.' He embarked on anecdotes about his thirty years in the business, the changes he had seen, the increasing influx of foreigners. It didn't take Lambert long to steer him from that to the Miszowski case.

'A couple of fellows in the pub,' he said. 'They were talking about it.'

'Yes, I remember the case,' the landlord said. 'She got off—but it was murder all right.' He gave a knowing nod.

'These chaps in the pub,' Lambert said, with doubt evident in his tone, 'they didn't think that, they thought it was a pure accident. One of them knew the husband slightly. He said he had a nasty side to him when he'd had a drink or two.'

The landlord shook his head with energy. 'That wasn't the way I heard it, not at all. That shipmate of Miszowski's, the one who went into the box and swore Miszowski was a jealous husband, used to knock her about for no good reason when he'd had a few—I heard he owed Miszowski money, quite a lot of money. They said he'd been told that in certain circumstances—' he half closed one eye—'Mrs M. would be prepared to forget about the money. And another thing I heard later, after the trial, when she'd married her solicitor and scarpered—'

He jerked his head suddenly upward at the sound of a bedroom door opening. A female voice called down, 'Harold!' with a note of iron.

He clicked his tongue and glanced at Lambert with an air of resigned irritation, stood up and opened the sitting-room door. 'Yes, dear,' he called up the stairs in a dulcet tone. 'I'll be up in a moment.' He came silently back and drained his glass. 'Drink up,' he urged. 'Got to dispose of the evidence.' He put the whisky away in the sideboard.

'What was it you heard?' Lambert said. 'After the trial?'

The landlord picked up the empty glasses. 'I heard she had a fancy man. The pair of them used to visit one of the pubs quite regular. After Miszowski was killed this fellow vamoosed, never seen or heard of again in these parts.'

'Did that come out at the trial?'

'It did not. Nothing came out at the trial that Roche didn't want to come out. But I'll tell you what I believe, and Mr Stephen Roche and all the tea in China won't alter my opinion.'

'What's that?'

'I believe she intended to marry her fancy man—but not by going the long way round, through the divorce courts. She was going to take a short cut and get whatever Miszowski had to leave into the bargain. Easiest thing in the world to kill a drunken man and who could prove he hadn't tried to attack her?'

'Do you think the boyfriend was in it with her?'

'No, I don't. From what I heard he wasn't the type. Some long-haired artist chap, we get a lot of them down here, they do quite well from the visitors. I don't know what tale she was planning to tell him about Miszowski's death, but whatever it was he didn't wait to hear it. The

COLD LIGHT OF DAY   145

moment he heard what she'd done he took fright and
bolted.' He laughed. 'I don't suppose she'd bargained for
that. But she came out of it all right in the end, that type
always does. There's always some fool of a man waiting to
take over from the last poor sod—till she gets old, of
course. But it'll be long enough before she has to worry
about that.'

CHAPTER 14

Lambert was up early next morning, wakened by the
landlord's cup of tea and two Marie biscuits, fare which
Lambert supplemented, as soon as the door closed again,
with a couple of Alka-Seltzers. As he drank his tea he contemplated the morning ahead; the first item on the
agenda might well be a visit to the offices of the local
newspaper, to look through the files of five years ago.

The landlady made her appearance the moment he
came downstairs. A powerfully built woman with a
resolute cast of feature, veiled now by a bright professional smile. Lambert assured her he'd slept soundly, his
bed was comfortable, his room left nothing to be desired.

A solitary place was set at the long table in the dining-
room. On the sideboard cereal packets were ranged in
regimented rows; Lambert shook his head as the landlady
gestured towards them.

'No, thanks,' he said. 'I don't think I'll bother this
morning.'

Her smile lost some of its candlepower. 'You can have
grapefruit,' she said on a faintly menacing note. 'Or
stewed prunes.'

'No, thanks,' he said again. 'Not this morning.'

'Very well then.' Her tone suggested that the gloves
were off now, she knew how to behave next. 'I'll bring in

your breakfast,' she told him like someone playing an untrumpable card.

She went swiftly off towards the kitchen and returned a couple of minutes later with an enormous plate, red-hot, entirely covered with food, every inch of it fried. Bacon, eggs, sausages, tomatoes, mushrooms, black pudding, fried bread. He could hear it all still sizzling.

'There you are then!' she said on a note of triumph. She plonked it down in front of him. 'That should keep you going till lunch-time.' Her husband brought up the rear with a tray of coffee and hot milk.

For one dreadful moment Lambert feared they were going to stand over him while he waded through the mountain of food but to his intense relief they departed, the landlord giving him a wink as he turned to close the door.

He glanced round the room in desperation. On a small table near the fireplace lay a folded newspaper. He crossed the room and picked it up; it was yesterday evening's. He drew some sheets from the middle, returned to his breakfast and swept the contents of his plate into the sheets. When he had made as neat a parcel as he could, he took off his jacket and concealed the bundle inside. He folded the attenuated newspaper and replaced it on the table, swallowed the last of his coffee and made a dash for it with the jacket under his arm.

As he reached the foot of the stairs the landlady suddenly appeared at the end of the passage. 'Finished already?' she said in a tone of keen disappointment.

He gave her a cheery grin. 'Yes, thanks. It was delicious. I have to rush, I'm late for an appointment.'

He reached the safety of his room and took the bundle from his jacket. As he stowed it away in his overnight bag, to be disposed of in the first convenient litter-bin, a paragraph in the paper caught his eye. He paused and read it. The opening of a new science block at Ryecroft School, a

photograph of the headmaster standing smiling outside
the building. Ryecroft—that was the school Osborne had
mentioned, where Stephen Roche had been sent after his
mother left home. I could pop over there after I've been
to the newspaper office, he thought. He wasn't at all clear
what he hoped to learn at Ryecroft but it would help to
fill in the morning. He needn't return to Cannonbridge
till the afternoon.

The offices of the *Kingsharbour Clarion* were in the old
part of town; the files were housed in the basement.
Lambert spent an hour reading the reports of the trial,
looking at the photographs. Mrs Sparrey in a dark
tailored suit, going into court, looking straight ahead, her
face disciplined into blankness; Stephen Roche coming
down the court-house steps, looking down, one hand in
his pocket, the other holding a briefcase; Annette as a
child in an airy ballet dress, her face full of vitality;
Annette as an eighteen-year-old bride in a wide-brimmed
hat and pale silk suit, smiling with open delight. And that
other photograph, the one that had stayed in Chief-
Inspector Kelsey's mind—a police photograph, blown up,
on a front page, under heavy black headlines: Annette
staring straight ahead, her hair taken plainly back, her
features rigid, her eyes expressionless.

There were several photographs of Miszowski at various
periods of his life; he was certainly a handsome man,
strongly built and vigorous-looking, with dark curly hair.
Lambert sat looking at the likenesses. Something about
the face that was vaguely familiar, reminded him of
someone he had seen recently. He studied them more
closely and suddenly it came to him, what they reminded
him of—the photographs of Gavin Elliott in the police
files at Cannonbridge.

The main building of Ryecroft School was a large early-

Georgian dwelling which had once been the home of a family that had in its day provided its quota of generals, admirals and lords-lieutenant of the county. Lambert, himself the product of a minor public school, felt a sharp twinge of nostalgia as he drove in through the handsome entrance gates, up the long drive, past a thick shrubbery of rhododendrons coming into bud.

His ring at the front door was answered by a uniformed maid. She was sorry, the headmaster wasn't available, but his wife—or the deputy headmaster—might be able to spare him a few minutes. Lambert chose the headmaster's wife and a few minutes later found himself in a small sitting-room stating his business to a competent-looking woman with a briskly friendly manner. He gave his own name but not his true profession; he declared himself to be an inquiry agent.

'I'm trying to trace someone,' he said, snatching yet another female name at random from the air. 'It's a matter of a legacy, nothing substantial, but the estate has to be wound up.' The mythical female had been left the money by an employer she had worked for thirty or forty years ago. 'It seems she left there,' he said, 'to take up a post on the matron's staff, here at Ryecroft School. I understand she left here a few years later. I wondered if there was anyone here now who could tell me where she went.'

'I'm afraid that was long before our time,' the headmaster's wife said. 'But I should be able to think of someone who might know.' She closed her eyes and tilted back her head. 'Mrs Tandy!' she said after a few moments. 'She was assistant matron here at one time, she left about twenty-five years ago, to get married. That was before our time too, of course, but I did meet her once, she came to an Open Day shortly after we came here.' She stood up. 'She married a parson, in a village about twenty miles from here.'

★

The drive was pleasant enough, little traffic and a fine sunny day. It was getting on for noon when Lambert approached the village. A church tower rose above a belt of dark green cypress; the rectory was near by.

Mrs Tandy was a plump, cheerful-looking woman in her fifties. Lambert disclosed himself again in the character of inquiry agent and explained that he was trying to trace someone she might have known years ago at Ryecroft School. She listened with interest to his spiel but couldn't help. 'I'm very sorry,' she said when he'd finished, 'I'm afraid I don't know that name at all, I must have missed her by a year or two.'

'We can always advertise,' Lambert said. 'We'll find her in the end.'

She offered him a cup of coffee and he followed her into the kitchen while she made it. 'Black, please,' he said, in deference to his still-aching head.

She took down beakers from a dresser shelf. 'I haven't been back to Ryecroft School for years now,' she said. 'I doubt if there'd be anyone left on the staff that I'd know. I'm kept so busy with the parish work and my family.'

'It seems a very good school,' Lambert observed idly. 'A man I came across not long ago in the line of business, he told me he sent his son there. Years ago, of course, that would be, the son would be a grown man by now.' He paused. 'Roche, his name was, he was a judge till he retired.'

'Roche,' she repeated on a considering note. 'Yes, the name does ring a bell.'

'The son would be thirty-seven or -eight now. Stephen, I believe his name was.'

'Stephen Roche.' She stood looking down with a little frown, then she suddenly raised her head and said with triumph, 'I've got him! A little fair-haired boy, very quiet. He came to Ryecroft very young, six or seven, he used to cry a lot at night.' She poured the coffee. 'Yes, it's coming back now.' She looked up at him. 'Strange creatures, children. I've had four of my own; I was an assistant matron for seven or eight years; I take the play-group three times a week; and still they surprise me.' She offered him biscuits but he shook his head.

She puckered her brows. 'There was something about his background—his mother had died or his parents were separated, I can't quite remember. Anyway, there was some domestic reason why he had to be sent to school so young. I don't believe in that myself, sending them away from home at that age. It's different when they're older, they're more stable, but six or seven—' She shook her head. 'They're not much more than babies. They can't understand what's happened, they think it's because they've been naughty, they've been sent away in disgrace. And if it's mixed up with the death or desertion of a parent, you can just imagine the emotional turmoil.' She had done her best to comfort young Roche, had made a point of saying a word, giving him a smile, whenever she could, going along to tuck him in and say good-night.

'He was very fond of me,' she said. 'I thought he was over the worst.' And then another child arrived at Rye-croft, a lad not much older than Stephen, with the same sort of reason for being sent away from home so young, sickness or death or parting, the same sort of reaction, tears and withdrawal.

'Of course I treated him in exactly the same way,' she said. 'I made the same sort of fuss of him, went along to say good-night and so on. He was in the same dormitory as Stephen Roche, the youngest children were all together.' One morning a week or so after the new boy arrived, she came across Stephen in a corridor. She stopped to have a smile and a word with him as usual. He didn't smile or chat in reply, he merely looked up at her with a stony face and said, 'There's no need for you to come and say good-night to me again, I don't need it any more.' She had stood staring after him as he went off along the corridor.

'He simply closed up against me after that.' Her look still echoed that old surprise.

The phone rang sharply in the hall and she went to answer it. Lambert finished his coffee. She came bustling back a couple of minutes later. 'That was my husband,' she told him. 'He's bringing the vicar of the next parish over to lunch.' She glanced at the clock. 'That gives me less than half an hour.' She snatched a pan down from a shelf. 'I'll have to leave you to find your own way out.'

It was turned six when Lambert reached Cannonbridge and drove on to the forecourt of the main police station. Chief-Inspector Kelsey was in his office.

'You're back then,' he said to Lambert, his thoughts clearly elsewhere. 'Come across anything?'

'A few odds and ends,' Lambert said. 'Nothing sensational.'

'Keep till morning, will it?'

Lambert nodded. 'Any developments here?'

Kelsey gazed back at him with an abstracted glance. 'We've got the loot, the Eastwood stuff.' It had been tied up inside a plastic refuse sack, dropped in an old flooded quarry in an isolated spot eight miles to the north of Littlebourne village. 'Some kids came across it. Mrs Cutler's seen the stuff, she's identified it. A few chips and scratches, but it's all there, nothing missing.'

CHAPTER 15

'I never did think much of the burglar theory,' Kelsey said next morning after Lambert had recounted his doings in Kingsharbour. Kelsey had listened with close attention but little comment and had immediately returned to the subject uppermost in his mind. 'I never could see a burglar stabbing Elliott to death in that way,' he said. Not in such a cleanly clinical manner; it had never suggested random panic—or generalized mania—to him. And the way the pyjama jacket had been turned back, that had always suggested someone who knew Elliott could be expected to be deeply sunk into an alcohol-induced slumber, someone who was determined to strike an exact spot, determined not to wound or incapacitate but to kill. 'Taking the stuff was just a red herring,' he said. 'It was only by the purest chance it came to light.'

Lambert wasn't ready to rule out a burglar completely. 'He could have taken fright when he realized what he'd done,' he argued. 'Decided to chuck the stuff away.'

'Then why take it out of the house? Why not just leave it at Eastwood?'

'He may not have panicked till after he'd driven away.'

'It was no burglar,' Kelsey said with finality.

Lambert knew better than to pursue the matter—for the moment, at least. 'At all events,' he said, 'it might seem to let Picton out. He'd have had to cycle sixteen miles there and back in the middle of the night, with that weight strapped on.'

'You can forget Picton,' Kelsey said. 'Stephen Roche faked the burglary after Annette told him she'd killed Elliott.'

'Anything to be learned from the plastic sack?' Lambert asked.

Kelsey shook his head. The sack was of the kind used by householders and local councils all over the country; any ironmonger or builders' merchant could supply one like it. The neck had been secured by a length of common twine. Some children fishing in the quarry had hooked the sack, convinced by its weight that they'd found sunken treasure — and even more convinced of their good fortune when they opened the sack and saw what was inside.

They had removed the contents and set them down on the grass, they had picked them up and examined them a score of times, had finally decided to take them home to show their parents. There the objects were again freely handled. If there had ever been anything useful to be got in the way of fingerprints, there certainly wasn't by the time the sack was eventually taken along to the nearest police station.

Kelsey got to his feet and began to pace about the office. 'Get over to the Northgrove Hotel,' he said. 'Find out if Roche got a phone call during that dinner.' He frowned fiercely down. 'And Mrs Sparrey — I'm damned sure she wasn't at home that Friday evening nursing Annette, because I'm damned sure Annette wasn't there to be nursed. Mrs Sparrey spent that evening doing what she usually does — and I very much doubt that it's sitting at home knitting, staring at television. A woman like that — never in this world. She was out somewhere enjoying herself, with a man, if I know anything. Pubs and clubs, that's her style.' He came to an abrupt halt. 'Get round them. Clubs first, then pubs, it'll be a club, I'll wager that. Find out if she visited any of them that Friday evening.'

At the third club he visited Lambert struck lucky. The place was almost deserted at this time of day.

'Yes, I know Mrs Sparrey,' the barman said. 'She comes in here a lot. Very handsome lady, always very pleasant.' He rubbed a cloth diligently over the counter; he didn't ask why the police should be interested in Mrs Sparrey.

'Does she come in on her own?' Lambert asked.

'No, always with a man. She usually sticks with one guy five or six months.'

'And the current guy?'

'A dealer, antiques, paintings, name of Beacham.'

'Do you know where he lives?'

'Somewhere north of Cannonbridge, not quite sure where. Country place, I understand, rather grand.'

'When were they in here last?'

'I couldn't say.' The barman picked up a glass and polished it vigorously. Lambert was aware that he had reached a point — and there was always such a point with barmen — where polite neutrality ceased and stone-walling began. He gave it one more try.

'Were they in here on Friday evening the week before last?'

'I'm afraid I couldn't say that either.'

Lambert wasted no more time. He left the club and found a phone-box. Yellow Pages listed Beacham under Antique Dealers, gave his address in a village seven or eight miles north of Cannonbridge.

He didn't need to ask for directions when he reached the village; two signs, a couple of hundred yards apart, gave him the information. He followed the arrows down a lane running between sternly disciplined hedges, past an orchard of cherry trees in bud. A gateway appeared on his right, bearing another sign. He turned in and found himself in a large square courtyard with a handsome Regency house set at right angles to the lane. A large estate car, newish, expensive, was drawn up by the front door. Lambert got out of his car and pressed the bell.

The door was opened almost at once by a woman in her late forties, thin and anxious-looking, with a pale skin, limp hair of a lifeless brown taken carelessly back from her face. She wore a nylon overall and had an air of chronic harassment.

'He's just going out,' she said to Lambert without preamble. Her tone was irritated, tinged with chronic mild hostility. 'I can show you round if you like, but if it's him you want to deal with, then you'll have to come back another time. He's just off to a sale.'

'I don't want to buy anything,' Lambert said when at last he was able to get a word in. He declared his identity and asked if he might speak to her husband, he wouldn't keep him more than a few minutes.

She looked at him in silence. 'I'll tell him,' she said reluctantly. 'He's not my husband, he's my brother.'

'Is there a Mrs Beacham?'

'There was, but they were divorced years ago. I've kept house for him ever since.' She left him standing outside while she went off. A couple of minutes later Beacham came to the door. A tall well-built man, not bad-looking in his way, three or four years older than his sister; he bore her only the slightest resemblance. He looked like a man who had struggled up from difficult beginnings and now had a secure foothold in the broad regions of the middle class. A well-cut tweed suit, good-quality shirt, a discreet whiff of expensive cologne. His expression was a good deal more relaxed than his sister's but his eyes were sharp and shrewd, missing nothing.

'I can't give you much time,' he said pleasantly. 'Would you like to step inside?'

He took Lambert into a sitting-room furnished with old pieces in a mixture of periods, arranged with care and skill, polished to a deep mellow shine. Military and sporting prints on the walls, a number of English water-colours; a great many objects in silver, jade, ivory. Everything manifestly for sale.

Lambert offered no explanations but asked him baldly if he had spent any part of Friday the fifth of March with Mrs Gertrude Sparrey.

A flicker of surprise showed on Beacham's face. 'Friday the fifth,' he repeated. 'That would be the weekend before last.' He paused to consider, then he said, 'No, I didn't see her that Friday, there was a big sale on that day.' He mentioned a large country mansion fifty miles away that had recently changed hands. 'I stayed to the end, I didn't get back here till after eight. By the time I'd unloaded and had a bite to eat, I was ready for bed.'

'Have you seen Mrs Sparrey since that Friday?'

'Have I seen her since then?' he repeated. He looked down at a Persian rug. 'No, I don't believe I have. I've been so busy lately, I hardly know what day it is, let alone— Oh, of course, I remember now, Gertrude's had her daughter staying with her, the girl's not well, Gertrude's been nursing her. I phoned her one day last week, she told me she wouldn't be able to get out for the time being, she'll be in touch again after her daughter's gone back home.'

'Do you know the daughter?'

'Never clapped eyes on her.' He glanced at his watch. 'I have to be going, I must get a look round before the sale starts.' His tone was briskly amiable, a reasonable man making a reasonable point.

'Right, then,' Lambert said. 'I won't keep you any longer.'

Beacham suddenly said, apparently as an afterthought, 'I hope Gertrude's not in any kind of trouble?'

'Not as far as I know.'

Beacham gave him a swift glance, saw that he wasn't going to enlarge. He went to the sitting-room door and called, 'I'm off, then,' down the passage. His sister came out through a door leading from the kitchen quarters. He brushed her cheek with his lips, gave her a pat on the shoulder and went swiftly off.

Lambert stood watching as Beacham drove out through the gate, then he walked over to his car. Miss Beacham remained in the doorway, looking at him. He halted and glanced across at her, then he walked back to where she stood.

'Has Mrs Sparrey been here lately?' he asked.

She looked surprised. 'Is that what you came to ask him? About Mrs Sparrey?' He gave a single nod. She stared at him for some moments with a fixed, intent look, then she said, 'She came over here about ten days ago, on the Monday evening, that was the last time she was here.'

'Was your brother expecting her?'

She shook her head. 'She rang up about eight o'clock, then she came straight over.'

'Do you know why she came?'

'No. I didn't speak to her, I just saw her arrive. I heard the car, I was upstairs in my bedroom, I came down right away. He must have been on the look-out for her, he'd already let her in. She didn't even look at me, they went straight along to the sitting-room and closed the door.'

'You don't like her?' Lambert said.

She jerked her shoulders. 'I've nothing against her, I hardly know her. I don't think she'd recognize me if she saw me in the street.' She gave a brief snort of a laugh. 'I'd know her all right, anywhere, could hardly fail to, she doesn't intend to be overlooked.' She gave him a piercing look, intense and vulnerable. 'He's always been like that, taken in by looks. He doesn't appreciate what I do for him. If he thinks a woman like that would do what I do here—' She gave a swift comprehensive glance around. 'I slave from morning till night. Not that I'd grudge it, any of it, if I was appreciated.'

She's terrified he'll marry again, that she'll be turfed out, Lambert thought. She'd probably seen half a dozen aspirants to the position of the second Mrs Beacham off the premises.

'Friday the fifth of March,' he said. 'Do you happen to recall if he went out with Mrs Sparrey that evening?'

'What did he tell you?' she said at once. 'Did he tell you he went out?'

He smiled. 'I'm asking you.'

She clasped her hands together. 'I couldn't say off-hand. I'd have to think about it.'

'Friday the fifth,' he said again. 'Did he go to a sale that day?'

He saw calculation run behind her eyes. 'I can't be sure. I'd have to look it up.' She suddenly added with a weary, deflated air, 'He doesn't tell me his business. Half the time he doesn't even tell me he's going out, let alone where he's going. I just hear the car.' He's learnt by this time, Lambert thought; better to keep his mouth shut, keep his private life to himself. He felt a twinge of sympathy for Beacham.

'He couldn't manage without me,' she said fiercely. 'I'm worth I don't know how much a year to him. On call all the time, any time anyone decides to drop in and take a look round, answering the phone, keeping everything looking its best. It's all skilled work, you know.'

'I'm sure it is.' Lambert turned and began to walk off again towards his car.

'They didn't go out anywhere that Monday,' she suddenly called after him. 'She was only here half an hour. He didn't tell me why she'd come, what it was about. But then I wouldn't expect him to.'

The Northgrove Hotel was in a somnolent afternoon lull when Lambert got over there. The manager was off duty and Lambert had to make do with his assistant, a young man not much over twenty, very keen, very anxious to oblige.

No, he hadn't been on duty on the evening of Friday the fifth of March, but he knew about the Chamber of Commerce dinner. They kept no record of incoming phone calls for dinner guests. Yes, the girl who was on duty at reception that evening was here now. It didn't seem to occur to him to ask why the police should want the information, he simply seemed pleased to help, like a schoolboy. He went with Lambert to reception, had a word with the girl and then took himself off.

The girl could offer little help. Yes, there had been some phone calls for dinner guests that evening; it would be a very rare function when that didn't happen. No, she never made a note of such calls, nor could she remember the name of any guest who had taken a call that evening. She smiled. 'I couldn't tell you any name from yesterday, let alone the best part of two weeks ago.'

Lambert went off again in search of the assistant manager and ran him to earth in the wine cellar. 'No luck,' Lambert told him. 'Perhaps one of the waiters might remember a phone call. Are any of them on duty now?'

The assistant shook his head. 'Not at this time of day. In any case I doubt if you'd have any better luck there. We take on extra help for functions, casuals from one of the agencies, or retired waiters, or men who're just friends or relatives of someone on the staff here, like to earn a bob or two in their spare time.'

No, they didn't keep a list of men they'd used on any particular occasion, and even if he could produce such a list, Lambert wouldn't be able to locate all the men on it instantly and with ease. 'They could come from anywhere,' the assistant explained, 'not just in this area. Some of these casuals work the whole country. And a lot of the arranging's done by word of mouth. You say to someone in the kitchen: How's Harry fixed for next Monday? Tennis Club dinner, six till twelve. A couple of days later you're told: It's OK, Harry'll be here. You don't know Harry's surname or his address. He's probably not even called Harry, it's just what he's got used to answering to over the years.'

CHAPTER 16

Gavin Elliott's funeral took place at eleven o'clock on Thursday morning. Howard Elliott had opted for cremation and the nearest crematorium was in a larger town some twenty miles from Cannonbridge. The funeral was as quiet as it was possible to make it, brief and simple, with a short service in the bright, airy little chapel attached to the crematorium.

No sightseers, largely because of the distance from Cannonbridge; no relatives, apart from Howard and Judith Elliott. The rest of the congregation consisted of members of staff from all three branches of Elliott Gilmore, and representatives of various clubs and associations. The Pictons were not there, nor was Mrs Cutler, nor Jessup, the Eastwood gardener; no member of the Neale family from Berrowhill Court was present.

The service seemed a curiously impersonal affair, conducted by a clergyman who had never set eyes on the dead man and who was a stranger to almost every member of the congregation. The only person who betrayed any emotion was Miss Tapsell; she burst into audible sobs when the coffin began its slow glide forward. The moment had no visible effect on Howard Elliott; he continued to glance calmly about as he had done throughout the service. Beside him Judith stared rigidly ahead. She was by far the most elegantly dressed woman in the chapel, in a slim black suit, a white lace blouse, and a becoming little toque of fine black straw, trimmed with airy puffs of veiling.

Kelsey had earlier run his eye over the floral tributes. Handsome, dignified and costly, wrought into elaborate shapes, but a certain sameness about them, as if they had all resulted from a single telephone call to Interflora. Nothing from the Neales. Nowhere among the offerings an uncomplicated sheaf or simple posy. Nowhere on the stiff black-edged cards anything that read like the expression of genuine grief or deep affection. Nowhere the name of a child.

In the afternoon Lambert drove the Chief over to Mrs Sparrey's house. Kelsey got out of the car and walked over to the boundary hedge. He stood looking down the garden. At the far end, beside some fruit trees, he could see a green shed. Closer to the house stood a timber garage with a small white car parked on the hard standing in front of it. Kelsey opened the little side gate and walked down to the garage; he peered in through the glazed upper half of the door. Inside was another small car, dark blue.

There was a sound of movement from the bottom of the garden. He glanced down and saw Mrs Sparrey coming out of the shed. She wore a shirt and slacks, and carried a pair of shears. As she turned to close the shed door she caught sight of Kelsey. She raised a hand and called out, 'Hello there!' Kelsey walked down the garden towards her. 'I've just been doing a quick tidy-up,' she said as he approached. 'I haven't been able to do much this last week or two. It soon starts to look untidy.'

'Your daughter's still with you?' Kelsey said.

She nodded. 'She's a good deal better, but the doctor says she'll have to be careful for some time, it's really taken it out of her. I'm keeping her here till the weekend. Her husband will be home then to keep an eye on her.'

'We'd like another word with you both,' Kelsey said. 'We won't keep you long.'

'Yes, of course.' She walked up the garden beside him with easy grace. 'Annette hasn't any help in the house now,' she told him. 'And Greenlawn's a fair size. It's all very well when you're feeling fit and strong, but a different matter altogether when you're not. I told her—and Stephen told her too—that it was a great mistake to let Mrs Broadbent go, she's an excellent worker.' She gave an impatient little shake of her head. 'But Annette would have it she didn't need her any more, she'd got the house the way she wanted it, it was a waste of money keeping Mrs Broadbent on, there wasn't enough for her to do.'

Kelsey glanced across at the small white car. 'Is that your daughter's?' he asked.

'No, it's mine. Annette's is in the garage.'

Kelsey nodded to Sergeant Lambert, who was still waiting by the gate, indicating that he should join them. They followed Mrs Sparrey into the house.

Annette was downstairs, resting in an easy chair in the sitting-room, with a rug wrapped round her. She looked somewhat better but still pale and tired. Kelsey asked after her health and then when they were all seated he turned to Mrs Sparrey and said without any preamble, 'Did you spend the evening of Friday the fifth of March with Mr Beacham, the antique dealer?'

She looked at him in silence, her face expressing nothing. Lambert saw Annette flick her a swift glance.

'No,' Mrs Sparrey said in a decisive tone. 'I didn't go out at all that Friday evening, I was in the house here from lunch-time onwards. Annette phoned around five or six to say she was coming over. I went upstairs and got her room ready, she came over right away. The only time I went out anywhere over the next few days was to slip down to the local shops for food.'

'Except for Monday evening, of course,' Kelsey said. She stared at him, at a loss. 'You paid a flying visit to Mr Beacham on Monday,' he said.

'Oh yes, I forgot that.'

'What was the purpose of that visit?'

She looked surprised. 'I can't see the drift of this. Mr Beacham is a friend of mine, we sometimes spend an evening together. He phoned me on the Saturday afternoon, that was the day after Annette came. He asked me if I'd like to go out with him that evening, but I was so busy, and so worried about Annette, I was rather short with him. I just said I couldn't go out, my daughter wasn't well. Afterwards I realized he might have thought me a trifle brusque. I wanted a breath of air on Monday so I drove over to see him and explain. I didn't stay long, I didn't like leaving Annette on her own.' She paused and then added, 'I can't see how any of this can conceivably be the concern of the police.'

Kelsey ignored the observation. He turned to Annette and said abruptly, 'Have you a key to this house?' She shook her head. 'Have you ever had a key to it?' Again she shook her head. He looked at her in silence for a moment, then he said, 'Have you a key to Eastwood?'

Mrs Sparrey gave a little gasp. Annette looked back at Kelsey, her grey eyes expressionless. 'No,' she said calmly. She remained quite still, her hands clasped loosely on her lap. A slow tide of colour began to rise in her cheeks.

'Have you ever had such a key?'

The colour rose steadily, relentlessly, it flamed right up to her hairline. She looked down at her hands folded on the rug. She gave a tiny shake of her head.

'You must see she's far from well,' Mrs Sparrey said in lively protest. Kelsey didn't glance at her, he kept his eyes on Annette's face. The colour began to drain from her cheeks, leaving her deathly pale.

'I will put to you a hypothetical case,' Kelsey said. 'A young woman, an attractive young woman, her husband is away a lot, she is bored and lonely. Without meaning to get involved in anything very serious, she drifts into an

association with a good-looking young man.' Annette
made no move. Mrs Sparrey looked as if she would utter
some sharp protest but then appeared to think better of
it.

'She gets into water a good deal deeper than she'd bargained for,' Kelsey continued. 'It remains a casual affair
on the young man's side but she falls passionately in love,
she becomes obsessed with him. He grows uneasy, nervous
about the whole thing, he wants to end the association.
She won't hear of that, she becomes distraught if it's even
mentioned. Things continue in this fashion, she growing
more demanding and possessive, he trying to retreat.
Then he meets a girl he believes is the kind of girl he has
been looking for, a girl who might make him an ideal
wife. He reaches a decision: he's not going to let this girl
slip from him because of a foolish association. He breaks
it off. But the woman won't accept that it's over. She
phones him, goes round to see him, argues with him,
broods over it, bitterly resents it.' Annette remained silent
and motionless, looking down.

'What has this farrago to do with my daughter?' Mrs
Sparrey asked in a tightly controlled tone.

Kelsey ignored her question. 'I suggest to you,' he said
to Annette, 'that it was not around six o'clock when you
arrived here that Friday evening, I suggest that it was
considerably later, several hours later.' She didn't look at
him, just shook her head in silence.

'Nonsense!' Mrs Sparrey said with force. 'I tell you
again: she arrived here shortly before six.'

Kelsey produced the knife and raincoat; he asked
Annette if she had seen either of them before. She gave
them a single horrified look and shook her head. 'You've
barely glanced at them,' he protested. 'Take a proper
look.'

Her mouth opened a little, her face wore an expression
of terrified revulsion. She gave them a second rapid

glance. 'No,' she said in a voice that was little more than a whisper. 'I've never seen them before.'

'It's possible,' Kelsey said relentlessly, 'that whoever killed Elliott wore the raincoat to protect his—or her—clothing against splashes of blood.' Annette looked as though she might faint, she put a hand up to her face. 'When the coat had served its purpose, the murderer threw it down over the body.'

Mrs Sparrey stood up. 'You must stop this,' she said in a voice of authority. 'I'll phone the doctor if you persist. You're going the right way about making her ill again.'

Kelsey looked up at her. She gave him back a fierce, unshaken stare. 'What about you?' he said. 'Have you seen either of these before?'

'I have not,' she said with force. Kelsey got to his feet and without another word left the house, with Lambert following.

'Annette did it all right,' Kelsey said as they reached the car. 'Her mother knows it, she's shielding her.' He struck his fists together. 'I'll break their story if it's the last thing I do.' He turned his head and looked up the road. Some distance away, on the same side, was a pair of semi-detached cottages; on the other side he could see the roof and chimneys of what appeared to be a fair-sized detached house standing at the top of a winding drive, set well back among tall trees. There were no other dwellings; the road ended in farmland. 'If Annette arrived here in the middle of the night,' Kelsey said, 'one of the neighbours may have heard the car.' He glanced at his watch. 'We can't stop now.' He had a mountain of stuff waiting for him at the station. 'You'd better get back here tomorrow morning, first thing, have a word with the neighbours.' He got into the car. 'And that cleaning woman, Mrs Broadbent, the one Annette Roche got rid of—she may have found out about the affair with Elliott, she could have seen or heard something. Annette didn't get rid of her without good reason. As soon as you've dropped me at the station you can get round to see her. That newsagent along the road from the Roches, he'll know where she lives. Cleaning women never live far from where they work.'

The newsagent and his wife were busy marking up the evening papers while their son sorted them into piles.

'Mrs Broadbent?' the newsagent said, barely glancing up from his task. 'Yes, I know her, she gets her papers here.'

'Number 9, Oxmore Terrace,' his son put in. A smart-looking, frank-faced lad, thirteen or fourteen. He gestured up the road. 'Two streets along from the next junction, turn left, it's on the right-hand side.'

Lambert found the house without difficulty. Mrs Broadbent took a minute or two to answer his ring. A plump, homely-looking woman in her middle forties. 'Yes?' She put up a hand and tidied away a lock of hair.

Lambert declared his identity and assured her he had no bad news to impart — for she stepped back at once with a look of distress. He asked if he might come inside for a moment; she might be able to give him a little information about a place where she had worked.

Her face cleared. 'Oh yes, do come in.' She held the door wide. She took him into a sitting-room on the left of the hall. The furniture had been pushed back and a length of brightly patterned material laid out on the carpet. Pieces of a paper pattern lay beside the material, some pieces were already pinned in place.

'You don't mind if I carry on with this?' Mrs Broadbent said. 'It's a costume for my youngest daughter. It's her dancing-class, they're giving a concert. I'm trying to get it cut out before they come barging in from school.'

'Go right ahead,' Lambert said. She knelt down and began pinning the rest of the pattern.

Lambert sat down. 'Some people called Roche,' he said.

'Oh yes.' She paused to run a finger down the instruction sheet. 'Mrs Roche, Greenlawn. I worked there till a couple of months back, three mornings a week.'

'Do you remember exactly when you left?'

'I certainly do,' she said with vigour. She picked up another piece and smoothed it into position. 'One week before Christmas.' She glanced up at him. 'And I didn't leave, not of my own accord. I was just told I wasn't wanted any more. I was never so flabbergasted in my life. I'd been there over two years and Mrs Roche had never given me the slightest sign she was thinking of getting rid of me.'

'You got on well with her?'

She picked up a pair of dressmaking shears and began to cut round the pattern pieces. 'We got on very well, never a cross word. She knew how she liked things done but she was never nasty about it, always very reasonable, always treated me with consideration.'

'And Mr Roche?'

She moved her head. 'I only saw him once in a way. But what I did see of him, he was always polite, never any disagreement, nothing like that.'

'They get on well together, the Roches?' he asked casually.

She paused in her cutting out and flicked him an upward glance. 'What's all this about?' she said on a higher, sharper note. 'Why are you asking these questions?'

'It may have some bearing on a case I'm working on. Nothing to do with you personally, I'm not in any way investigating you.'

She seemed vaguely reassured, she bent again to her work. 'As I say, I didn't see them together very often but as far as I know they get on well enough.'

'How did Mrs Roche come to dismiss you?'

'She just said she didn't need me any more, she'd be able to manage the house on her own now. It was when she was paying me at the end of the week. She thanked

me for all I'd done, said she appreciated it very much, I'd
helped her to get the house the way she wanted it.'

'What did you say?'

She gave a brief snorting laugh. 'I couldn't say anything much, I was knocked sideways. Apart from anything else I needed the money at that time of the year, I
was counting on it. But what could I do? She was within
her rights. I did say: Is it something I've done? Or not
done? Just tell me and I'll put it right, whatever it is. But
she said: No, it's nothing like that, it's just that I don't
need the help any more, I don't feel I can justify the
expense.'

'Perhaps that was it,' Lambert said. 'Maybe they were
getting strapped for cash and her husband asked her to
economize.'

She cut out the last of the pieces. 'It didn't look to me as
if she was trying to economize. Only the day before she'd
come back from a sale with her mother—they go to a lot
of sales together, Mrs Roche more or less furnished
Greenlawn from sales. Mrs Roche had bought a little
china group, pretty enough but not as big as your hand. I
know what she paid for it because I heard them talking.'
She sat back on her heels and looked up at him. 'She'd
given a hundred and twenty-five pounds for it—and she
thought she'd got a bargain.'

CHAPTER 17

Early next morning Lambert drove the ten miles over to
Mrs Sparrey's neighbourhood again. There was no sign of
activity about Mrs Sparrey's house as he drove past and
parked his car outside the pair of semi-detached cottages.

He walked up the path of the first cottage and pressed
the bell. No reply. He pressed again, a third and fourth

time, without result. He gave up and went next door. Here his ring was answered almost at once by a spry old man, bright-eyed and alert-looking. Lambert disclosed his identity, hoped he wasn't calling at an inconvenient moment, asked if the old man could help him in some inquiries he was making locally.

'Yes, of course, anything we can do to help,' the old man said cheerfully. 'Step inside, my wife'll want to be in on this. We don't get out much now, it can get a bit dull sometimes.' He led the way along the hall, into a kitchen where a frail-looking old lady was sitting at the table eating a boiled egg. She glanced up with a friendly, lively look.

'Do you know who we've got here?' her husband said with the air of one springing a welcome surprise. 'A detective! Come to ask if we can help him.'

Her eyes shone with pleasure. 'Find the gentleman a chair,' she instructed her husband. 'Offer him a cup of tea.'

Lambert asked if they could cast their minds back a couple of weeks, if they could recall hearing a car arrive at the house at the top of the road, at any time during the late afternoon, evening or night of that Friday.

They looked at each other, they sought to recall and identify the day, they offered suggestions to each other, withdrew them, offered fresh ideas. Lambert listened without hope. 'It's the night I'm particularly interested in,' he said. 'Perhaps you were wakened by the sound of a car?'

After another involved exchange with his wife the old man shook his head regretfully; they'd certainly have remembered if they'd been wakened by any unusual sound in the night.

'Do you know Mrs Sparrey?' Lambert asked. 'The lady in the end house?'

'Not really,' the old woman said. 'We know who she is

of course, we know her to say good morning to, but that's about all.'

'Would you know if she had her daughter staying with her?' No, they wouldn't know.

'Your next-door neighbours—' Lambert said as he stood up.

'They're away,' the old man told him. 'They've gone to Spain for a month.'

'How long have they been gone?'

'Three weeks.'

When Lambert left, the old man stood in his doorway, eagerly watching. Lambert gave him a wave as he got into his car. He turned into the main road and saw a milk-float five hundred yards ahead, the milkman standing beside it, refilling a crate. Lambert sounded his horn and the man glanced round. Lambert raised his hand and pulled up behind the float; he got out of his car.

'If I could have a word with you,' he said as he came up. He declared his identity. Did the milkman deliver at Mrs Sparrey's? Yes, he did. Had he been delivering extra milk there recently? Yes, he had, he had also been delivering extra cream, eggs, yogurt, bread, potatoes and fruit juice. 'She's got her daughter staying with her,' he said. 'She's been poorly, bronchitis or something.' He looked at his watch. Friday, money to be collected. He resumed his crate-filling.

'When did you start delivering these extras?' Lambert asked.

'On the Saturday.' He screwed up his eyes. 'Two weeks ago tomorrow, that would be.'

'Had Mrs Sparrey told you she was expecting her daughter?'

He shook his head. 'No, she'd paid me the day before and she never said anything then about her daughter. She told me on the Saturday her daughter had come over un-expected, she'd had to put her straight to bed, she was

running a fever.' He grinned. 'She said: "It's their
mothers they come running to when they're not well,
married or not." '

Towards the end of Friday afternoon there was a message
for the Chief from Berrowfield Court, Mrs Neale ringing
to say that Charlotte would be returning from Switzerland
that evening.

Before nine next morning Kelsey and Lambert were on
their way to Berrowhill. The Chief stared out of the car
window as they approached the village. No shortage of
cash in the Neale coffers, it seemed; a fair-sized farm as
well as the racing stables. The land looked in good heart;
in the orchards damson and pear trees breaking into
blossom.

The clock in the tower of the stable block showed nine-
twenty when they reached the Court, a seventeenth-
century manor house in a superb state of preservation.
Mrs Neale received them in a small sitting-room. A tall
woman, bony rather than slender, with large, well-set
eyes, a longish jaw and longish nose, thick dark hair
sprinkled with grey, taken back into a classic knot low on
her neck. She had an air of diffuse goodwill overlaid with
a certain abstraction as if part of her mind was on something else—as indeed it was; her husband, a man of many
interests, was in the habit of suddenly taking off in pur-
suit of one of them, leaving her to grapple with the rest
till his return.

'I'm sorry my husband's not here,' she told the Chief.
'He's in Ireland.' Looking for bloodstock—and good
company. 'I'll tell Charlotte you're here.' She drew a little
sigh. 'What a dreadful business, poor young Elliott.' She
paused on her way to the door. 'He and Charlotte were
not particularly close, they hadn't known each other long.
She liked him, but there was no more to it than that.'

When she had gone the Chief crossed to the window

and stood looking out at the paved terrace with its great screen of lilacs that would be a spectacular sight in May. The door opened again and he turned from the window.

Mrs Neale came into the room with a young girl in the fresh bloom of her beauty. Oh, I don't wonder Gavin Elliott made up his mind the moment he clapped eyes on her, Kelsey thought. He would surely wish to be rid of all foolish encumbrances to be free to woo this flower of the English counties.

He explained the necessity for taking her fingerprints and neither she nor her mother offered any objection. 'I expect you'd like to talk to Charlotte alone,' Mrs Neale said when Lambert had finished. 'I won't be far away if I'm wanted.'

When the door had closed behind her Charlotte said, 'It was a horrible shock. I couldn't believe it, I still can't.' She gave the Chief a level look. 'I didn't know Gavin very well. I went out with him a few times, that was all.' There was no trace of a tear in her beautiful lobelia eyes; her voice, hands, manner, were all perfectly steady.

She had last seen Gavin the evening before she left for Switzerland, they had dined together at the Caprice. He had had a cold, it seemed to get steadily worse during the evening, she had told him to take care of it. Apart from that he had seemed as usual—but she hadn't known him well enough to be able to spot if there had been something troubling him that he wasn't talking about.

Kelsey asked if she knew anything of any previous attachment of Gavin's, recent or more distant, but she shook her head; he had never talked about anyone.

She hadn't visited Eastwood very often. 'We went back there once or twice after we'd been out for the evening,' she said. 'And one Saturday morning, when we were going to a race meeting, he picked me up here and drove me back to Eastwood, he wanted me to see the garden. We had some coffee and then we went off to the races.'

'Did you ever drive over to Eastwood yourself?' Kelsey asked. 'In the evening?'

She looked surprised. No, she had never done so, she had never had any reason to do so. She gave the Chief another glance from her brilliant blue eyes, candid and direct. 'We weren't on those sort of terms.' Nor could she add anything useful to what they already knew about his way of life.

'The relationship seems to have been straightforward enough,' Kelsey said to Lambert as they walked out to the car. 'It certainly doesn't seem to have got very far.' He got into the car and sat frowning out at the vast sweep of the garden; he whistled a few notes through pursed lips.

'Something that occurred to me,' Lambert said. The Chief continued to frown out at a bank of rhododendrons, continuing his erratic tune. 'Howard Elliott,' Lambert said, undeterred. 'Do you think he was aware of the Roches' history?' Kelsey stopped whistling. 'It's Howard who benefits from Gavin's death,' Lambert said. 'Benefits very considerably. What keeps coming back to me is this: Why did Howard go back to the family firm? He'd been seventeen or eighteen years with another firm, he gave up whatever expectations he had there. For what? To remain number two to Gavin for the rest of his working life? I can't see him being content with that. Until he was twenty-three years old he believed he was an only child, and then to have this interloper inherit—there must have been a terrific build-up of resentment over the years. The only motive that makes any sense to me is that he went back in order to secure his rightful inheritance, one way or another.' He paused. After a moment he said, 'And to do that, Gavin had to die. And die while he was still single.'

Kelsey chewed the inside of his cheek.

'But Howard is so obviously the one who benefits by Gavin's death,' Lambert continued, 'that he would have to do everything in his power to blur that one central fact—so we have the attempt to make it look like a burglary. Then there's Picton, Howard knew about him, about the quarrel, that would be another useful red herring. And if in addition he knew the Roches' history— that would strike him as a tremendous piece of luck. If he mimics the manner of Miszowski's death, it will all help to confuse the issue.'

Kelsey still said nothing; he stuck out his lips in a fierce pout.

'There's not a shred of evidence against Annette,' Lambert said. 'Just an echo of an old case, old prejudice. We don't even know that there was anything more than sheer accident in her husband's death, everything else is invention or speculation, gossip, rumour, spite. She was, after all, acquitted by a jury. None of her fingerprints were found at Eastwood, you have no proof she'd been having an affair with Elliott. There's no proof he'd been having an affair he didn't want talked about, with anyone at all—except the tale of a lying, attention-seeking child. But if Howard knew Annette's history, he'd know that sooner or later her fingerprints would reveal the old story—and we'd jump to conclusions on the strength of that.'

Kelsey continued to frown out in silence through the windscreen.

'Howard could have gone to the Northgrove dinner,' Lambert said, 'but he chose not to. I believe he went along to Eastwood instead. There was no one to see him come or go at either house. He knew the sort of state Gavin was likely to be in.'

There was a brief silence, then Kelsey suddenly slapped his knee and said briskly, 'No, I won't have it. It was Annette who did it.' Lambert saw the angle of his jaw. Knowing there was no point in continuing, he sat in silence waiting for the Chief to decide on his next move.

Kelsey put up a hand and massaged his cheek. 'If Roche did get a phone call from his wife or Mrs Sparrey at the Northgrove dinner,' he said, 'what did he do then? Did he drive straight over to Eastwood or go back to his digs first?'

'He was definitely at the dinner till around midnight,' Lambert said. 'No doubt about that. And his landlady says he came in about twelve-fifteen, she saw him and spoke to him.'

'Then he went straight to his digs from the hotel. He changed out of his dinner-jacket, gave the landlady the impression he was going to bed, waited till she fell asleep, then he went quietly downstairs and let himself out of the house. He comes silently in again an hour or two later, he tiptoes up to his room, she's none the wiser.' He performed some elaborate facial exercises. 'Right, then!' he said after another minute or two. 'We'll get over to Martleigh now. We'll have another word with his landlady.'

CHAPTER 18

The drive to Martleigh was short in distance but high in irritation. Lambert was forced to halt three or four times because of the roadworks; once they sat waiting for ten minutes while Kelsey fumed and frowned. 'I don't wonder Roche went into digs in Martleigh,' he said when they were under way again. 'Twice a day of this sort of thing in the rush hour would be enough to drive a man barmy, with a day's work sandwiched in between.' He stared out at the traffic. 'Not much of a life in digs—but I dare say Roche can afford a decent enough place. What's she like? His landlady?'

'Struck me as a nervous type,' Lambert said. 'Hypochondriac. Getting on a bit, aches and pains.'

'Sounds a bundle of fun.' Kelsey cast his mind back. 'Mrs Nugent, isn't it?'

'Yes. She hasn't been widowed all that long, eighteen months or so. She's probably quite jolly in the ordinary way.' They came to a junction and Lambert turned left. 'She lives down here.'

When they reached the house Kelsey sat regarding the property for a minute or two before he got out of the car and walked along the adjoining street. He glanced over the wall at the long back garden. A lawn, a rockery, some fruit trees, a garage at the far end with a short drive leading out into the side-street. He turned and stood looking up at the rear of the house, then he rejoined Lambert and they walked up the path to the front door. Lambert pressed the bell.

There was a sound of movement inside the house and a few moments later the front door opened a little. Mrs Nugent peered round it with an anxious look. Her hair had been newly done, the curls were even crisper and tighter, tinted a richer shade of brown; the treacherous tinge of white had vanished from the roots.

'Good morning, Mrs Nugent,' Lambert said in a cheerful, bracing tone. 'You remember me? Sergeant Lambert. We had a chat the other day.'

'Yes, I remember.' She looked no whit less anxious.

'Chief-Inspector Kelsey would be glad if you could spare him a moment,' Lambert said. 'It's nothing to worry about.'

She frowned. 'I'm really on my way out—it's just that I've been waiting for the phone.'

'We won't keep you many minutes,' Kelsey said with massive reassurance.

'I thought we'd finished whatever it was the other day,' she said to Lambert with baffled irritation.

'Just checking one or two little details,' Kelsey said. 'I don't think the sergeant can have got them quite right when he was here before.' He pulled out his notebook and stared at imaginary notes. 'These young men,' he said in a tolerant, confidential tone, 'always in too much of a hurry to be accurate.' He stabbed a finger at a page. 'A mistake here, right off. He's given your age as in your sixties.' He gazed at her with a bland smile. 'That's never right, for a start.'

She gave a pleased little smile and opened the door a fraction wider. 'Oh, but it is,' she said. 'I'll be sixty-seven in June.'

Kelsey allowed a look of amazement to flit across his craggy features. 'Never!' he said with gross and unabashed flattery. 'I'd have put you down a good ten or fifteen years younger than that.' He gave her a winning smile. 'If we could just step inside. We won't keep you many minutes, not if you're on your way out. We wouldn't want to hinder you.'

'All right, then.' She held the door wide. 'It's my daughter-in-law,' she said in a sudden surge of words as they stepped over the threshold. 'She's expecting her first, it's due any moment now, she's not been at all well. They've been married twelve years, I thought I'd never have a grandchild, but they managed it in the end. They live up north, they're all the family I've got. She's been in hospital since tea-time yesterday. I've got to go out to the shops but I didn't know whether to hang on or not.'

'It's a worrying time for you,' Kelsey said soothingly when at last she paused for breath. 'But it'll be over soon, I'm sure you'll have good news.' He glanced round the hall. 'This is a very nice property you've got here. Nice quiet neighbourhood too.'

'Oh, it's quiet enough,' she said. 'A bit too quiet sometimes. I got nervous living here on my own after my husband died.' She twisted her wedding ring. 'That's why I decided to take a lodger.'

'Very wise too.' Kelsey glanced up the stairs. 'I expect

you've got a wonderful view of the river from that landing window. Mind if I pop up and take a look?'

'No, not at all.' She was beginning to look marginally less anxious.

Kelsey went up the stairs with Lambert behind him. After a moment's hesitation Mrs Nugent followed them.

Kelsey reached the window and glanced out at the distant gleam of water. 'I thought so.' He turned and smiled at her. 'Mr Roche is lucky to find such pleasant digs. I expect he's got a good big room. That's the best of these old properties, plenty of space.'

'That's his room.' She pointed along the landing. 'And he has a sitting-room downstairs.' Her manner was more relaxed now.

Kelsey strolled along the corridor and opened the door of Roche's room. It was immaculately tidy. 'Oh, my word, yes,' he said. 'Very pleasant.' He stepped inside and Lambert followed him. Mrs Nugent came along and stood in the doorway.

'That evening Mr Roche went to the trade dinner,' Kelsey said. A bird shrilled suddenly outside the window. Mrs Nugent uttered an exclamation and jerked her head in the direction of the downstairs hall. 'Oh, I'm sorry,' she said a moment later. 'I thought I heard the phone. What were you saying?'

'The evening Mr Roche went to the dinner at the North-grove Hotel, did you speak to him after he came back?'

'Yes, I did. I'd gone to bed—that's my room, along there.' She gestured at a front bedroom. 'But I couldn't settle, I never can till the house is locked up for the night. I'm a very poor sleeper now, I have been ever since my husband died. I've got my pills, of course, but this last couple of nights I haven't dared take them in case my son rang up about the baby. I'm going round all day half asleep, worn out, I don't know whether I'm coming or going.'

'Did you take a pill that Friday night?' Kelsey asked.

'Oh yes, it's only this last couple of nights I've stopped. I took one after I'd spoken to Mr Roche, when I knew everything was properly locked up. I slipped on my dressing-gown when I heard him come in, that would be about twenty past twelve. I went along and knocked at his bedroom door. I asked him if he'd had a good evening and he said yes, very good. I asked him if he'd locked up and he said he had. So I wished him good-night and went back to my room and took a pill. They're marvellous, they knock you right out.'

'He'd still be in his dinner-jacket,' Kelsey said jovially. 'When you knocked at his door.'

'Oh no, he was in his dressing-gown.' She put up a hand and stifled a yawn. 'With a sweater on underneath,' she added in a tone of half-attention.

'A sweater?' Kelsey echoed. 'I'm sure he wouldn't need to go to bed in a sweater, not in a nice warm house like this.'

'No, of course not. But he did have a sweater on, I remember distinctly. I didn't pay much attention at the time, but I can see him now, standing in the doorway with his dressing-gown pulled tight round him, and a roll collar at his neck—brown, it was, a sort of heathery mixture.'

'I expect it's a sweater he wears a lot,' Kelsey said idly. 'You're mixing it up with some other time.'

She shook her head. 'I've never seen that sweater before—or since, come to that.'

'Do you know,' Kelsey said suddenly on a matey note, 'my tongue's hanging out for a cup of tea. And I'm sure the sergeant could do with one.'

She gave a little laugh. 'I wouldn't mind one myself, now you mention it. I'll go and put the kettle on.' She went along the corridor towards a rear staircase.

Kelsey's demeanour instantly underwent a marked

change. He moved swiftly and silently about the room, stooping, stretching, examining, peering, opening and shutting. He carried a straight-backed chair over to the wardrobe and stepped gingerly on to the chair. On top of the wardrobe was a suitcase. Behind it, folded down into a well, was a zipped holdall of some soft synthetic material.

Kelsey lifted down both cases and opened them. The suitcase was empty. Inside the holdall was a plain green paper bag containing a man's sweater, roll-necked, new-looking, expensive, a brown heathery mixture. He removed the sweater and the bag and replaced both cases where he had found them. He stepped down from the chair and thrust the bag at Lambert. 'Shove that up your jumper,' he said. Lambert stuffed the bag inside the waistband of his trousers and buttoned his jacket over it; it gave him a paunchy, middle-aged look.

Kelsey turned his attention to the dressing-table. He opened the two long drawers and ran his hand expertly through them. Everything was very tidy, neatly folded; when he closed the drawers again the contents looked undisturbed.

On either side of the oval swing mirror of the dressing-table was a tier of three small drawers holding various oddments, rolled-up ties, dress studs, cufflinks, aspirin tablets, sticking-plasters, safety-pins. In the middle drawer on the right, under some handkerchiefs, was a jeweller's box, dark blue; no name on the box. Kelsey sprang open the catch. Inside, on a bed of cream-coloured velvet, lay a pair of silver drop ear-rings, delicately fashioned in a circular filigree design, inset with the stylized figure of an archer.

Lambert bent his head to look at them. 'Sagittarius,' he said. 'Annette Roche's birthsign. Could be an anniversary present, the Roches were married in April.'

From the foot of the rear staircase Mrs Nugent's voice

called up to them. 'Tea's ready!' Lambert stuck his head out and shafted his voice along the corridor. 'Right, thanks. We'll be down in a jiffy.'

Kelsey snapped the box shut and thrust it into his pocket. He closed the drawer and Lambert replaced the chair. They left the room and went along the corridor and down the back stairs. On the right a door led out into the garden; on the left was a utility area opening into the kitchen. Mrs Nugent was pouring the tea. She made inquiries about milk and sugar; she was looking anxious and harassed again.

'I'm afraid I haven't any cake,' she said in a distracted fashion. 'But I've got some biscuits.' She looked about uncertainly, then went to a shelf and took down a tin.

'Does Mr Roche get many phone calls here?' Kelsey asked idly.

She looked at him as if only just recollecting his existence. 'No, not many,' she said after a moment. 'He gets the odd one.'

Kelsey took a biscuit. 'That evening he went to the dinner—did he get a phone call here that evening?'

She looked down at the floor. 'I don't think so, I can't remember one.'

'Did he get a call after he came in from the dinner?'

'Oh no!' she said at once. 'He's never had a call as late as that. I'd certainly remember if he had.'

'What about the following morning? Before he went to work?'

'No, I don't think so. I don't think there's ever been a call for him at that time of day. Oh, I wonder why my son doesn't ring,' she added in a little wailing rush. 'He could at least let me know what's going on. Do you think I should phone him?'

'I doubt if he'll be at home,' Kelsey said. 'He's probably at the hospital. But I'm sure you've no need to worry. This time tomorrow you'll be on top of the world, celebrating, wondering what on earth you were so worried about.'

She smiled suddenly. 'I do hope you're right. Wouldn't it be marvellous? Do you think perhaps I could pop out and do my shopping?'

'Good idea. It'll take your mind off things.'

'Right,' she said with decision. 'That's what I'll do. I'll just wash up these cups and then I'll go.'

Kelsey drained his tea. 'We'll get along then, out of your way. Thanks for the tea. And the chat.'

Outside in the car Lambert took the paper bag from inside his jacket and handed it to Kelsey. The sweater carried no store mark, just a manufacturer's label; a high-class garment of a well-known English make that might be bought in any good outfitter's or department store.

'Forensic,' Kelsey said. 'We'll get over there and let them take a look at it.' He dropped the bag on the dashboard shelf, leaned back and closed his eyes.

As Lambert let in the clutch he heard the phone begin its ring inside the house.

CHAPTER 19

It was turned three when they approached the eastern edge of Cannonbridge on their way back from the laboratory. Lambert halted the car outside Greenlawn and the two men walked up the sloping drive.

Annette Roche's car was standing by the open front door; Mrs Sparrey was reaching into the boot. There was a sound of a female voice and Annette came out of the house, saying something to her mother as she came. She walked with a light, brisk step, she looked better, more animated. Her chestnut hair gleamed in the sunlight; it looked freshly washed, carefully dressed. At the sound of their approach she turned her head. Her look of animation vanished, she came to an abrupt stop.

'Good afternoon,' Kelsey called out. Mrs Sparrey straightened up, she turned and looked at them, her face expressionless. 'Is Mr Roche at home?' Kelsey asked. 'We'd be glad if he could spare us five minutes.' Annette remained where she was, in the same frozen posture.

'I'm afraid he's not here,' Mrs Sparrey said in a voice of easy apology. 'He's with Howard Elliott, they're down at the Cannonbridge office, getting things sorted out. I shouldn't think he'll be long.' She didn't glance at her daughter. In spite of her relaxed manner Lambert had an odd feeling that she was fiercely on guard, that if they took a single step towards Annette Mrs Sparrey would suddenly fly out at them in some deadly attack.

'In that case,' Kelsey said amiably, 'perhaps we could come inside.' He glanced at Annette. 'We'd like another word with you.' She made no reply, didn't move.

'Yes, of course,' Mrs Sparrey said after a perceptible pause. She went towards the house and the two men followed her. As she reached the steps Annette roused herself. She turned and without speaking or looking at any of them went inside, just ahead of her mother.

Good Lord, she's lovely, Kelsey thought, staring after Annette, riveted by that beautiful fluid movement, that long, slender seductive waist. She wore a simple, closely fitted woollen dress, with a narrow belt loosely encircling, lightly defining. Mrs Sparrey, in well-cut slacks and tailored jacket, was graceful and elegant, but there was about her movements and the proportions of her figure an indefinable suggestion of the long lapse of years since her magnificent youth.

'If you'd like to come in here,' Mrs Sparrey said as if she were the mistress of the house. All four of them went into a sitting-room on the right, furnished with considerable taste and discretion, no single piece especially fine but everything chosen with care, harmoniously arranged.

Mrs Sparrey offered to make them coffee but Kelsey declined. 'I'd like a word with your daughter on her own,' he said pleasantly. Mrs Sparrey glanced at Annette who sat looking down, her hands folded in her lap. She didn't return her mother's look and after a moment Mrs Sparrey said, 'I'll bring in the rest of the things from the car.'

When the door had closed behind her Kelsey said to Annette, 'I must ask you again what time you arrived at your mother's house that Friday?'

She didn't change her posture, didn't look up at him. She said in a low clear voice, 'Round about six in the evening.'

'Would you swear to that in court?'

She gave a single nod.

'I put it to you,' Kelsey said, 'that at some time last year you formed an association with Gavin Elliott.' She remained looking down, and shook her head in silence.

There was a sound of voices outside, Mrs Sparrey's and another voice, a man's; Kelsey recognized it after a moment as Roche's. Annette gave a little sigh, leaned back and closed her eyes.

A few moments later Mrs Sparrey and Roche came into the room. Mrs Sparrey glanced at Annette but said nothing, remaining standing just inside the door. A flicker of anger crossed Roche's face. He went over to Annette and put a hand on her shoulder. She didn't stir, they didn't look at each other.

'Is this necessary?' Roche asked Kelsey with a sharp edge to his tone. 'You know my wife is convalescing.'

'I don't think I've been unduly harsh or pressing,' Kelsey said mildly.

There was no softening in Roche's manner. 'If you have any further questions to ask my wife,' he said, 'I wish them to be asked in my presence.'

'I'll bear that in mind,' Kelsey said equably. 'Perhaps

you'd answer one or two questions yourself while we're here.'

'Very well.' Roche's face expressed weary irritation. He glanced down at Annette. 'I'll take the Chief-Inspector into the study,' he told her. He touched her arm. 'Try to rest.'

He led the way down the hall into a smaller room on the left, equipped with a desk, bookcases, hide armchairs.

Roche sat down in the swivel chair, half turning so that one elbow rested on the desk. He raised a hand and supported his forehead on the outstretched fingers, looking down at the flat leather top of the desk. Lambert settled himself into an armchair but the Chief chose an upright hard-backed chair a few feet away from Roche who sat motionless, in silence, waiting for the Chief to begin. Kelsey took his time about it.

'When you left your lodgings around midnight that Friday,' he said at last in a flat neutral tone, 'and drove over to—'

'I did no such thing,' Roche interrupted with force. 'I drove back to my lodgings from the Northgrove Hotel and went straight to bed.'

'Why did you put on a roll-necked sweater to go to bed?'

Roche smiled slightly. 'I packed my suitcase before I went to bed, ready to take with me in the morning because I was driving home from the office. I suddenly remembered the sweater—it was a Christmas present from my wife. The last time I was home she asked me where it was, I never seemed to wear it.' He smiled again, removed his elbow from the desk and sat back in his chair. 'To tell the truth, I'd forgotten I had the sweater. I'd brought it over here, thinking I might wear it in the evenings, then I put it away and never gave it another thought. So I looked it out and tried it on, I slipped it on

over my pyjamas. Mrs Nugent came along to speak to me.
I put on my dressing-gown and went to the door.'

'Forensic tell me,' Kelsey said in the same colourless
tone, 'that the sweater was at some time worn underneath
the raincoat that was thrown down over Elliott's body.'
Forensic had also told him there were no bloodstains on
the sweater; it had never been washed or dry-cleaned.

Roche frowned. He looked at the Chief with fierce concentration, he tilted back his head and stared up at the
ceiling. Suddenly he leaned forward and slapped his
knee. 'Got it!' he said with triumph. 'That must have been
the raincoat Miss Tapsell lent me.' He jerked his head.
'Yes, that must have been it.' He spoke with animation. 'I
wore the sweater one Friday afternoon when I went over
to Cannonbridge for the weekly meeting. During the
meeting I found I needed a file, I'd left it in the car. It
had come on to rain rather heavily. I said I'd go and get
the file and Miss Tapsell said: "You'll be soaked." She
said there was an old raincoat, she'd go and fetch it.
When I went outside I held the coat over my head and
ran across to the car.' He moved his shoulders. 'I'd forgotten the incident. I didn't know whose raincoat it was
or where she'd brought it from.'

'Forensic tell me,' Kelsey said, bland and dispassionate,
'that the raincoat was at some time actually worn over the
sweater, not just held over the head of someone wearing
the sweater.'

Roche smiled again. 'Forensic are quite right. When I
got the file out of the car the rain had slackened off a bit,
so I slipped the coat on and held the file inside it, under
my arm, to keep it dry. When I got back inside Miss
Tapsell brought me a towel to dry my hair.'

'Did you take the raincoat home with you?'

'No, I gave it back to Miss Tapsell as soon as I took it
off.'

'You're sure of that?'

'Quite sure.'

'When did this incident occur?'

'Last autumn sometime. September or October.'

'I understood you to say the sweater was a Christmas present.'

'It was. Not last Christmas, the Christmas before.'

'Do you often wear a casual sweater to the office?'

'No, I don't,' Roche said lightly. 'I sometimes wear one on a Friday afternoon if I'm going over to the meeting in Cannonbridge. I'm not dealing with clients then, I always go home after the meeting.' He gave a brief laugh. 'I would never have worn a sweater in old Matthew's time, not on any day of the week.'

'You're very fond of your wife,' Kelsey said. Roche made no reply but regarded him levelly. 'I believe you'd do a very great deal for her. Are you quite sure you wore that sweater on that day in the circumstances you have just described?'

'Quite sure.' Roched glanced at his watch. 'Is there anything else?' he said with an edge of impatience. He swivelled his chair a little.

'The phone call you received towards the end of the Northgrove dinner—'

Roche ceased swivelling. 'Phone call?' he echoed sharply. 'I received no phone call.'

'I was under the impression you did,' Kelsey said calmly. 'I understood you were called to the phone sometime towards midnight and that you left the hotel immediately afterwards.'

'That's total rubbish,' Roche said with force. 'Or sheer invention on your part. Who led you to understand it? Who gave you the information? There was no such call.'

'I understood the call was from a woman. Mrs Roche. Or Mrs Sparrey.'

'You understood nothing of the kind,' Roche said with vehemence. 'There was no such call.'

'Was your wife having an affair with Gavin Elliott?' Kelsey said in the same even tone.

Roche uttered a sound of anger. 'That's a monstrous suggestion!'

'She never confessed such an affair to you?'

'She most certainly did not.'

'You never saw or heard anything to suggest such an affair?'

'I certainly did not.'

'I believe you would go to considerable trouble to protect your wife from the consequences of her own folly,' Kelsey said. Roche made no reply. 'Is there anything you would not do to protect her? Is there anything you would not cover up for?'

'I've never covered up for her,' Roche said.

'Never?'

'Never.' He looked steadily back at the Chief.

Kelsey suddenly stood up. 'I'll be back in a moment.' He flicked a look at Lambert to remain where he was.

When he had gone Roche turned without haste to his desk. He opened a drawer and took out some papers. He began to look through them with an air of total concentration, picked up a pencil and made some marginal notes. He was still engaged in this when Kelsey came back into the room a few minutes later, accompanied by Annette and Mrs Sparrey.

The faces of both women were closed and expressionless. They sat down in silence, close together, Mrs Sparrey upright and tense, Annette leaning back in her chair; neither woman looked at Roche, who ceased to work on his papers. He didn't turn round from his desk but sat looking down at his hands.

Kelsey walked across to the window and stood leaning against a cabinet. 'Have you any hobbies, Mrs Roche?' he suddenly asked in a bright conversational tone.

Annette looked startled. 'I'm interested in antiques,'

she said hesitantly. 'Particularly in porcelain. And interior decorating generally.' Lambert saw that Roche was covertly watching his wife but it was impossible to read his expression. Mrs Sparrey stared straight ahead at the opposite wall where a marine oil painting hung facing her.

'Any outdoor hobbies?' Kelsey asked on a rallying note. 'Any sports?'

'Only gardening,' Annette answered with the same uncertain air. 'I used to play tennis at one time but I gave it up.'

'You do a fair amount of gardening?'

She gave a little nod.

'At all seasons of the year? You're not just a fair-weather gardener?'

She nodded again, she seemed baffled by his line of questioning.

'How do you dress for it?' he asked in a briskly matter-of-fact tone. Mrs Sparrey moved in her chair and gave him a swift glance. Roche remained perfectly still, watching his wife. Annette looked at the Chief with a hypnotized air.

'I usually wear trousers,' she said after a little pause. 'With a shirt.'

'And a sweater if it's chilly?'

'Yes.'

The air in the room had an electric quality; they were all as rigid now as waxworks.

'Do you ever borrow one of your husband's sweaters?' The words seemed to drop one by one, like beads.

There was another pause before she answered, 'Yes, sometimes.'

'Have you ever called in at the Cannonbridge office of Elliott Gilmore?' Kelsey said with one of his swift changes of tack.

She blinked. He's beginning to get to her, Lambert

thought. She was starting to swallow in little convulsive jerks. After a moment she said, 'Yes, I have, but not very often.'

'When was the last time you called in?'

'It was some time ago. Before Stephen went to Martleigh.'

'Did you ever have occasion to borrow a raincoat while you were there—if it suddenly came on to rain, perhaps?'

There was total stillness in the room. She shook her head slowly.

'You're certain?' Kelsey persisted.

'Quite certain.'

'Have you ever worn a raincoat that your husband brought home from the office? Worn it even for a few minutes? To pop out into the garden, perhaps?'

She shook her head.

'Do you remember him bringing a raincoat home? One he'd borrowed from the office?' Again she shook her head.

'You would swear to all this in court?'

There was another, longer silence, then she said, 'Yes.'

He's obsessed with her, Lambert thought. All three of them are telling the truth but he won't see it. Howard Elliott's the one, he killed Gavin. They're all dead now, everyone involved in the treachery against his mother: his father, his father's mistress, their son; the entire inheritance is back in his hands, the hands of the original successor. The whole of that episode is now wiped out as if it had never been. His mother can rest in her grave.

CHAPTER 20

Kelsey turned his head and glanced out of the window. Down the road, away to the right, he saw the lad from the local newsagent's on his round. He reached Greenlawn and jumped down from his bike; he stood looking at the cars, then up at the house. He wheeled his bike to the gate and propped it against a pillar, took a newspaper from the bag slung over his shoulder and started up the drive.

Kelsey turned from the window. 'I'm going down to the car,' he said. 'I won't be a moment.' He went rapidly from the room, out through the front door and down the drive. He met the newsboy coming up, whistling, taking his time, stopping to peer into a cranny in the ivy-covered stones of the bank, where a wren was building a nest. He turned his head at the sound of Kelsey's approach.

'Oh—hello,' he said, recognizing the Chief, who sometimes came into the shop. He gave Kelsey a sharp look that clearly asked: What's up? What are you doing here? But he knew better than to voice the question. 'I saw the cars,' he said. 'I thought Mrs Roche might be back, she might be wanting me to start leaving the papers again.'

'When did you stop leaving them?' Kelsey asked.

'Two weeks ago yesterday, after Mrs Roche spoke to me. She said she'd let me know when she got back from her mother's.'

'At what time did she speak to you that Friday?'

'When I came up to drop in the evening paper, that would be about a quarter past five. I'm later on weekdays because of school.' He gave the Chief another glance of lively curiosity.

'What was Mrs Roche doing when she spoke to you?'

'She was putting some things in her car, by the front door. She had a terrible cold. She said she was going to her mother's for a few days. She told me not to leave any more papers, she'd call in at the shop when she got back, she didn't know how long she'd be away.'

'Did she say anything else?'

'Yes, she asked me what time I'd be going past there again on my way home. I said about half past eight, I was calling in to see a mate after I'd finished the round. She said: "In that case, I wonder if you'd do me a favour." I said: "Sure, if I can." She said she'd ordered some stuff from a nursery a few days back, some roses and shrubs, they told her they delivered on Friday evening, after the nursery closed. The van wouldn't get here till about seven or eight and she didn't want to hang on that long. Her husband wasn't coming home till next day and she didn't want the stuff left outside the back door all night. She asked me if I'd call in on my way home and put the shrubs in the shed, cover them with sacking. I said sure, no trouble.'

'Did you do it?' Kelsey asked.

'Yes. I called in here about a quarter to nine. The stuff was outside the back door. I carried it across to the shed and put the sacks over it.'

'Did you see any lights on in the house? Was there anyone about?'

'No, no one. It was all closed up and dark, everything quiet. I went off home.'

'Right,' Kelsey said. 'I don't think you need bother Mrs Roche just now. I'll take the paper. Someone'll call in at the shop and let you know about delivering again.'

The lad went back down the drive and jumped on his bike. Kelsey stood in thought for a moment, then he went down to the car.

A few minutes later he let himself into the house again. Judging from the silence in the study and the attitudes of its occupants, no one had moved or spoken since he'd left. He laid the newspaper down on a small table without explanation. He took his original seat, close to Roche and the two women.

He produced the heather-mixture sweater in its plastic envelope and held it out. 'Have you seen this before?' he asked Annette.

She nodded, her face full of tension. 'Yes, it belongs to my husband.'

'Have you ever worn this sweater?'

She shook her head. 'It's too new, I wouldn't wear one of his good ones for gardening. I gave it to my husband for Christmas.'

'Christmas which year?'

'This last Christmas.'

'When is your birthday?' he asked abruptly.

The sudden switch seemed to throw her. She flushed, then her colour ebbed away, leaving her very pale. She looked immeasurably fatigued.

Mrs Sparrey glanced at her with acute concern. 'I really think she should go upstairs and lie down,' she said to Kelsey with a note of appeal.

He made no reply but kept his eyes on Annette. 'When is your birthday?' he asked again.

She looked vaguely about as if trying with an immense effort to recall the date. She'll collapse if he keeps this up, Sergeant Lambert thought.

'November the twenty-fifth,' she said at last.

'Sagittarius?'

She gave a tiny nod. She looked drained and ill.

Kelsey suddenly dipped a hand into his pocket. He leaned forward and brought his closed fist to within a few inches of her face. He sprang open his fingers. 'Yours, I believe,' he said. 'Given to you by Gavin Elliott.' On his palm lay the ear-rings he had taken from the drawer in Roche's dressing-table.

She jerked back with an involuntary movement; she looked terrified. She flicked a glance at her husband; he was watching her with fixed ravaged intensity. As their eyes locked Kelsey saw a look of naked vindictive triumph, malicious challenge, flash across Roche's face. Annette drew a little sobbing breath. Then the look vanished, Roche wore again his expression of concentrated attention.

Kelsey felt the hairs prickle along the back of his head. He heard the startled gasp Mrs Sparrey gave.

'You!' he said to Roche. 'It was you killed Elliott!' There was total silence in the room. Roche looked at the Chief with a steady gaze.

'Elliott gave you the ear-rings for your birthday,' Kelsey said to Annette. She gave a little trembling nod. 'You had to keep them hidden away among your things, away from your husband's eyes. You could wear them only when you were alone with Elliott.' She gave another nod, barely perceptible.

'Something had aroused your suspicions about your wife and Elliott,' Kelsey said to Roche. 'You felt driven to search among her things, looking for evidence. You came upon the ear-rings. Ear-rings you had never been shown, that she had never mentioned to you. You were sure Elliott had given her them—why else would she hide them? You were certain now they were having an affair. You removed the ear-rings, took them over to Martleigh, kept them in your lodgings.' To brood over in the solitary evenings, fuel his bitter resentment, his savage sense of betrayal.

'You waited to see if your wife would say anything when she discovered the ear-rings were missing. But she said nothing, made no mention of their disappearance. If you had any lingering doubts they were gone now.' He glanced at Annette. 'When you found the ear-rings had vanished you concluded Mrs Broadbent must have taken them. You daren't openly accuse her, you simply dismissed her.' Annette lowered her head; her hair swung forward, hiding her face.

Roche sat in silence; he continued to regard Kelsey with the same unwavering gaze. 'Perhaps you looked for further proof,' Kelsey said. Easy enough to phone Greenlawn at unexpected times, checking if Annette was at home when she said she was, setting little traps for her, catching her out in untruths and deceptions; easy enough to drive over from Martleigh in the dark winter evenings, keep watch unobserved on comings and goings, building up the evidence, stoking his own passion for revenge.

'You didn't confront your wife or Elliott,' Kelsey said. 'It wasn't a showdown you wanted, you had decided on another course of action. You took your time, laid your plans. You removed Gavin Elliott's old raincoat from the cleaning cupboard in the basement, a garment you could safely abandon at Eastwood when it had served its purpose, protecting your clothing against chance splashes of Elliott's blood. You took the raincoat over to Martleigh, kept it in readiness.

'You sat tight and waited for the right moment. The affair between your wife and Elliott had already come to an end but either you weren't aware of that or it made no difference to how you felt, what you had decided to do. When Elliott phoned you at midday that Friday, you knew the moment you were waiting for had come.'

Annette put her hands over her face and began to sob, a low muffled sound. Mrs Sparrey went across and sat on the arm of her chair, she put an arm round her shoulders; her face wore a stunned, dazed look.

Kelsey stood up. 'I must ask you to come down to the station,' he said to Roche in a formal tone. Roche made no reply. He looked down at the papers on his desk, gathered them up and put them neatly back in the drawer. He got to his feet and stood in silence, looking straight ahead, his face wiped clear of expression.

'I'm afraid I must ask you to come as well,' Kelsey said to Annette. Mrs Sparrey glanced up at him with a sharp exclamation. 'It's all right,' he assured her. 'She'll have to make a statement, but we won't keep her any longer than we have to.'

'I'll come with her,' Mrs Sparrey said.

When they came out of the front door a little later the air smelled fresh and sweet. At the turn of the path Roche paused for a moment and glanced back at the house, then he resumed his steady pace, between the two policemen.

They walked down the drive towards the cars. Lambert watched Annette walking ahead beside her mother, with that lovely fluid grace. There'll always be another man, the Kingsharbour landlord had said over the empty whisky glasses; someone to take over from the last poor fool.

A wren alighted on a branch of a shrub, his beak festooned with wisps of straw. It suddenly occurred to Lambert that tomorrow was the first day of spring.